The Blessing

Responsibility to Redemption

(The Your Vibe...Now Mine Paranormal Shifter Romance Trilogy, Book 1)

By

Adah Kennon

ISBN: 979-8-9881193-1-9

Edited and Formatted by Self-Publishing Services LLC.

www.SelfPublishingServices.com

Dedication

Dedicated to Almighty God and my spirit guides who honored me with a glimpse into their beautiful world of possibilities.

Epigraph

"To thine own self be true." Hamlet, Act 1, Scene 3

Table of Contents

Prologue

Newly formed sprites that tumbled from the eyes of The Almighty found refuge in Lias' outstretched arms. Eldest deity of all second plane colonies, he tenderly cradled each as he crisscrossed colony after colony in search of a tribe with space enough to care for one more.

Satisfied, he begrudgingly left his charge to be reared in one of the tribes' grooming places throughout infancy, childhood, and adolescence. That would keep their energy fields well-defined and keep them safe until the coming-of-age ritual.

The ritual was a routine event held each year to celebrate a sprite's transition into full status as a deity, with a true calling and destiny of his or her own. Many would become light workers, perhaps residents of first plane. Others would choose a different path. There was no reason for Lias to suspect this upcoming ritual would be any different than the others. That is, until the day he was contacted by the only deity in the Heavenly Realm with higher status than his own.

The voice was all too familiar. It was smooth like black velvet, baritone, warm but firm. Hearing it caused the silver layers of Lias' energy field to dance with a glow brighter than starlight as he exclaimed, "To what do I owe this honor, my Lord?"

"What we discussed long ago has finally come to pass. My children are being persecuted. The voice of one who makes false claims and offers empty promises has caused discord and confusion. The birth pangs of a new Sun City have begun; and, as above, so below on planet Earth. Is Ra ready to receive the blessing?"

Lias paused and thought, *Ra as your champion? Ra as the vessel to retrieve the secret that restores the gift that will end the persecution of your children? Any one of his peers at the ritual would be more qualified to carry-out your wishes.*

"You've changed the process, my Lord?"

"Yes. If things go as I plan, it won't be necessary for me to attend the next ritual."

Lias shook his head in regret. *I haven't seen you since you gave our plane deities the responsibility of cultivating within each sprite a desire to appreciate the benefit of a close relationship with you. It's always nice to hear your voice, but I hoped you would make a personal appearance at the ritual. There were so many things I wanted to impress you with, like my understanding of the nature of emotions and feelings and the importance of taming the beast within through logic, control, and discipline. The need must be great for you to miss a ritual gathering.*

"Uh, my Lord, Ra's not quite…ready. He hasn't been cleansed. Like the blade of a sword that's being forged, his character still needs…tempering. You always said that, if necessary, the choice would be made during the ritual. And we've always prepared for such a time. But…".

Lias' words faded into silence as he considered the situation. It wasn't personal, but he never thought Ra would amount to anything special. The sprite was more of an irritant. There was something different about him. Ordinary as he was, he could be stubborn and preoccupied. His rebellious nature challenged well-honored expectations. Conform? Rebel? He never confronted Ra about it. He just hoped a miracle would help tradition win the day.

"Honestly, my Lord, he's preoccupied with a desire for things he'll never experience in the Heavenly Realm. Oh, he's a dreamer alright. Self-serving, a thrill-seeker, not at all practical minded. Adventure. Excitement. He hasn't learned how to tune out distractions. If you're willing to settle for that, then he's a good choice. But if something more is required, like discipline or good judgment, then there might be problems." Lias' voice grew insistent. "Ra won't know what to do. Give me time to cleanse him, especially when it comes to temptation. He hasn't faced it, let alone conquered it. To confer the blessing prior to the ritual will awaken a passion within him that might only be one of many possible callings. You might be disappointed."

Lias sighed and thought, *You expect Ra to put someone else's vibe above his? He's never performed a noble or positive act that involved service to others over self-interest. Yet you expect him to do just that, and without cleansing?*

The voice paused, then continued. "Lias, you forget that cleansing can take many forms. I understand your hesitation but I have my reasons."

"I'm sorry, my Lord. I know there is purpose in all you do. Anyway, you always get what you want."

A soft restrained burst of laughter filled the space of a long second. "Sometimes I don't. It's true he hasn't been cleansed. Perhaps the seductive allure of vibes different from his own will invade and corrupt his energy field, lure him from the path I choose for him. There are always possibilities. However, I'll make you a bet."

"A bet, my Lord?"

"That won't happen. He will step into and claim the power I gave him before he tumbled from my eyes. Service to others over self-interest. Yes, he will choose to do this, in fact, many times over. He will understand that his true calling is also his destiny. In fact, he will not only satisfy every requirement necessary to be worthy of the blessing, but also for membership in the League of Stewards, the elite group of deities I formed to create universes and realities."

"All this before attending the ritual?"

"Yes."

"And, my Lord, if successful…the covenant you have with our colonies?"

"My favor and protection will continue."

"What if Ra chooses a different path?"

"I would never stand in his way if he decides to venture out on his own in a different direction. I've given him free will, but he must make the choice. As my chosen vessel, his test of faithfulness to me demands that his true calling also be his destiny. However, if he chooses a calling other than the one, I chose for him, he will forfeit full status as a second plane deity and the covenant will be broken. I would naturally be disappointed and compelled to reconsider certain privileges afforded the colonies of your plane, like my favor and protection. But…let's not dwell on the negative. Have faith. Send Ra to me and don't tell him that we've talked or who I am. Just tell him you've been informed of an opportunity, a position he might qualify for in Sun City."

Lias hoped nothing would ever jeopardize the covenant that existed between The Almighty and second plane colonies since the beginning of time itself. However a bet was still a bet. Relieved to be free of his burden, he smiled and thought, *The matter is out of my hands. Ra will be your responsibility. You have already chosen the path he will follow and judging from the edge in your voice, there seems to be some urgency about getting on with it.*

"One thing, my Lord. If you find Ra unworthy, if you find any imperfection in him, uh…you won't hold that against me, will you? I mean, well, I certainly wouldn't want to be blamed for ending such a splendid relationship."

"Would I hold you responsible for something you personally had no control over?"

"No," Lias replied thoughtfully.

"And Lias …"

"Yes, my Lord?"

"Please don't worry. When the student is ready, the teacher will appear. Whatever happens, blessings be upon you, my most faithful steward."

Part 1 - Lynette

Chapter 1

- Entry Level Position Opening
- Creator God Apprentice
- Pathway to a future filled with Adventure! Excitement! Perks!
- Minimum Requirements:
  - o Loyal.
  - o Reliable.
  - o Able to conduct honest self-appraisals and seek corrective measures, when necessary.
  - o Team player.
  - o Follow instructions.
  - o Willing to learn.
- Second plane full status deities only.
- No prior experience necessary.

Contact: The Almighty, Great Creator God
Building Number One
Karoonsville Field Office,
District A (West Side), *Sun City*

Ra couldn't have been more surprised when Lias pulled him aside and informed him about the job opening.

"An entry level position as a Creator God Apprentice. What a wonderful opportunity for you! You'll be well ahead of the others in Jacinth, your tribe's grooming place. And who knows, there might even be additional honors in store for you if you go to the ritual having already performed a noble act."

We've had our differences, thought Ra. *But this is totally out of character for Lias. I'm the least qualified of all my peers, so why is he bringing this wonderful opportunity to my attention?*

Ra studied the fine print, then raised a question about one of the particulars. "Excuse me, sir, but it says that only second plane, full status deities need apply?"

A little bead of sweat popped out in the middle of Lias' forehead. He quickly swiped it away and mumbled, "Well, uh, that's probably a mis-print. You've got a lot going for you. Just show up for the interview and see what happens."

Ra raked his fingers through his closely cropped, jet-black coils, hoping it would take his mind off the low, deep, raspy voice that by now had become a familiar visitor in his mind.

"I didn't invite you to break into my thoughts," he muttered.

"But here I am." The cocky note in the low, deep, raspy voice was unapologetic. "Did you hear what Lias said? Noble acts. Well, I suppose. But this is the offer of a life time! Excitement, adventure, and a chance to experience the mysteries that have always called to you. The day you land that job will be your lucky day. You'll make those old second plane elders take you seriously. They've kept sprites ignorant about so many things far too long. The second highest position in Sun City? Why, the honor alone will ensure your admission into the League. You'll become a legend, the first sprite to bridge the gulf between unquestioning obedience and contact with outsiders before the ritual. You'll show others that future success without compliance is possible. Go ahead, thank him. THANK — HIM!"

Ra lifted his chin and flashed Lias a smug little smile. "Whatever you think is best, sir," but his tone was less than sincere. "Thank you for the opportunity." *As far as I'm concerned, the job is already mine. Showing up for the interview is just a formality. What could possibly stand in my way? Truth? If the purpose of truth is to gain respect and get what I want, then I'll do what I always do — make sure I have no faults. After all, lies are just little fibs that promote my own best interest and arrogance. Well, that's just confidence. Existence in this dwelling place is dull enough. I can't wait to get to that interview.*

Chapter 2

Sun City, first plane capitol of the Heavenly Realm and home to light worker deities. Once dubbed The City of Light and Love, it had become a paradox of contradictions.

Ra was beside himself as he followed the directions Lias had given him. *I'm finally on my own*, he thought. Like a stranger in paradise, there were few things he failed to notice.

Two buildings loomed in the distance. One was a four-story structure that glowed like a luminous citadel. The other was a rather unremarkable-looking single-story structure, slate-gray, surrounded by a spiky wire fence. It peeked-out from behind the taller building.

Ras' gaze fixed on the taller building as he thought, *That must be* Building Number One.

The facade of the taller structure was majestic and embellished with gemstones, brilliant and rare, the kind found only in the City.

Ra suspected he was close to his destination. Chest out, shoulders squared, chin raised up, head held high. What began as an easy gait became a serious stride with a cocky, overconfident attitude.

When he finally stood by the sign that read Field Office, his suspicion was confirmed. He paused for a second at the door, then opened it. When he crossed the threshold, Ra found himself in a lobby that had a welcoming feel to it. Pleasantly spacious, it seemed curiously unoccupied by anyone but himself.

The lobby connected into two corridors: one on the right and one on the left. Not knowing which one to take, he searched for any marker that might put him on the correct path. Nothing to be seen, with one exception. One large red arrow flashed on a dimensional wall panel directly behind the huge reception desk that sat in the middle of the lobby. That caught his attention. The arrow pointed in the direction of the corridor on his left. From where he stood, Ra could see it ended in a flight of stairs. Hoping it was the correct choice, he decided to follow.

He climbed up one flight to the second floor, stood there and quickly surveyed the area. A small placard rested on a metal stand. Field Office, The Almighty, Great Creator God.

This must be the place, he told himself.

The huge space he was about to enter was divided into at least two parts with a few nooks and crannies not readily visible from his vantage point.

Ra craned his neck to get a better view. Several unoccupied folding chairs, arranged theatre style in consecutive straight rows were in the rear section.

The front part was some kind of reception area. Sparsely furnished, there was a small desk that had a thick wood top the color of oak and perched on lighter black metal legs. An armless wooden chair, the same color as the desk, with casters and a seat-adjustment lever, was pushed into the kneehole. A small sign was taped to the front of the desk: Will Be With You Shortly.

There were only three things on the desk: a traditional physical telephone with a series of push-button lights; a standard, manual typewriter; and, a little silver call-bell. When shaken, the dry air in the building made its clear, resonant ringing sound much louder than needed to attract attention. There was no security to stop him. So, Ra casually strolled over, shook the bell, and piped, "Hello? Is this where I check -in?"

A presence, female, was hunched down a few feet behind the desk. At the sound of the bell, she rose, ever so slowly and turned to face him. Coming to a standing position, she hesitated for a second.

Did I frighten you? he wondered, as he studied her hazel eyes, large as full moons with flecks of gold at the center.

Suddenly she walked closer to the desk and faced him. Ra sensed that she was a deity, albeit lower in status than himself. His inquisitive gaze took in all that was visible about her shimmering ethereal form.

Ra studied the way she was dressed. *There's something almost unassuming about her,* he thought. *Not too showy. Everything polished. I'll bet it's in compliance with the company dress code. Black tailored pencil skirt secured around her slim waist in back by a zipper…open slit in front just long enough to expose the top of one knee. A long-sleeved, buttoned-down white silk blouse with a high collar accentuated with a bow. Plain black closed-toe pumps with heels, probably just high enough to comfortably run around the office in.*

She's tall, possibly just under six feet. Looks like the color of her skin—ochre, deep brown highlighted with red and flecks of yellow—continues into the bubbles of her soft yellow energy field. Coarse, jet-black hair, swept up and held in place at the back by a little golden comb. How quickly she smooths the one unruly strand come loose back in place.

Ra felt his heart rate quicken and breathing get a little faster. He inhaled a quick breath, then released it in a silent whistle and thought, *After work hours, I wonder what her body might look like?*

"Yes, say in a black gossamer dress, classic…sultry… with a neckline that plunges far enough to show cleavage…a *lot* of cleavage, and an above-the-knee hem-line short enough to show-off her legs. I'll bet they're toned, long and slender."

The low, deep, raspy voice in his mind was back.

This time Ra tried to dismiss it as being his imagination working overtime. But sending it away wasn't going to be that easy.

"Oh, come on sprite. You don't have any real experience with females. No male deity has. You just dream about what it would be like to enjoy the affection of a scantily clad female. Play your cards right and maybe one day I'll...*enlighten* you."

Chapter 3

Clean-up someone else's mess. That's what the temp thought as she let out a long sigh and surveyed the scattered piles of paper that cluttered the floor behind the desk. The regular front-desk receptionist was out for the day on another assignment, but took time to leave a note for her stand-in: Make sure the contents of each file only contains the appropriate paperwork based on an applicant's proper name as printed on the file label.

Proper name. Having one for herself was now just a distant memory. At least that was the reminder she received from her inner critic.

But there was a time when everybody knew that Lynette was her proper name.

Back then she was known as a go-getter, one of a handful of deities who held the high-status title of Administrative Assistant. She had a home with the company, the place where she could show her true self without hesitation or apology.

A bright light shined within her essence back then. The required skills came easily to her. She had faith and began each day with a positive statement about her ability to achieve anything she wanted, go as high as she wanted. *I am pleasant and accommodating. I can work under pressure, multi-task, problem solve.* Of all the things she was good at doing, she enjoyed serving others the best. It sent glittery pink splashes throughout the soft yellow bubbles of her energy field, something that didn't go unnoticed by those around her. That confirmed what she did was her true calling, and also her pre-ordained destiny. It had to be. Another voice—smooth, deep velvety and baritone, somewhere inside of her essence whispered it was so. She had come to think of that voice as her faithful encourager. Who was she to disagree?

The promise she showed was envied by coworkers, especially a male she shared a vibe with who left her for greener pastures. She didn't regret the good times they shared or the pleasurable spinning sensation in her head that made her feel like she was about to pass out that engulfed her essence as he bragged about the role he played in secret company projects best forgotten.

A casual comment made by another, a false accusation of betrayal. That was all it took for him to abandon her, turn on her, and circulate a rumor that she was a whistle-blower who couldn't keep her mouth shut about things she couldn't possibly know.

Unless he told her.

Protection. Romance. Empathy. Recognition. All denied. Instead, she was set-up to fail and when it happened, judged harshly. Word got around. No one came to her defense. The bright light within her essence dimmed, left her with deep emotional scars and a painful reminder to keep her mouth shut. She lost her top-secret security clearance, and with it access to all the dirty little secrets the company tried to keep a lid on. Things that made her shiver, yet crave more of. Things that when leaked guaranteed her popularity among those she mingled with. Things that kept her up way past midnight, high on an adrenaline rush, wondering how long she, and others she knew, would be safe.

Her demotion to the status of temp regrettably sent every part of her life spiraling on a downhill slide. She became suspicious of everything and everyone. When her plea to the voice, her faithful encourager, was met with silence, insecurity replaced confidence. That, and a very bad case of the jitters, nagged at her to constantly watch her back.

Rejected. Humiliated. Disgraced. Discarded. Saddled only with assignments no one else wanted. Now at the bottom of the heap, she was devastated. That's when she lost her proper name and settled for being referred to as she, her, or the temp. She faded into the background and became comfortable. As happened with the light within her, she had become almost…invisible.

But the light didn't go out entirely. Dim as it was, it was still somewhere within her essence. Something within her refused to let her stop dreaming of the day when she might regain her proper name and status within the company, repair her reputation. And finally get a good night's sleep.

Until then there was safety in keeping a low profile. Invisibility was a deception of her own making, and working as a temp was where she found it.

Temps were wanderers. Never belonging, never in one place long enough to stumble upon classified information which, if exposed, would put superiors in compromising positions. With low-level clearance, temps were never assigned any really important responsibilities. Rarely spoken to, they never came in contact with management.

She dreaded being judged by others. But eventually she learned to live with the burning and churning that came with those stomach-tied-up-in-knots upsets. She followed orders, hid her curiosity and untapped native ability in hard work with small-scale tasks, justified a comfortable level of mediocre performance far below her potential, and told herself it was a small price to pay if it meant she might get called back, even if only as she, her or the temp.

The company made sure each temp was familiar with the visitor check-in process. Each was given a copy of the greeting script. Official, detached. She played it over and over in her head, probably too often. Other than that, no one had rehearsed any visitor scenario with her. No appointments were scheduled on the roster. With no security guards around, this deity's presence made the acid in her stomach churn. In the back of her mind she wondered, has the building security system been breached? Is this deity a threat to me? She had a job to do, but needed to remain alert to take action at the first sign of trouble. For now, she stood there, watching him watch her.

Chapter 4

It wasn't that Ra had a problem with service to others over self-interest. He just didn't have the discipline or control to resist the temptation of an alluring female who might be open to his advances.

Especially when the low, deep, raspy voice inside his head egged him on.

He watched the temp and thought, *She's so fine.*

"What do her vibes tell you? She's probably no higher than a third plane deity. Just look at where she's working. In a Field Office, an unsecured space. All alone and at the mercy of anything that might breach the boundaries of her energy field. Protection. Status. Security. Land this job and see what happens when you take her places she could never go on her own."

Ra hadn't mastered the technique of keeping the boundaries of his energy field as well-defined as possible. Opening himself to her would make him vulnerable, subject to undesirable infiltration or an unhealthy energy transference.

He had a decision to make: was going after her worth putting himself in harm's way?

The low, deep, raspy voice in his mind piped up with a resounding, lustful, "Yes, sprite. Why not? You never know what might happen. Consider it practice for a future main event. Go ahead. Experiment. Treat her any way you desire. Let her serve you. Bend her to your will. She's already given you an invitation…eyeballed you like a piece of candy. She's nothing special to you, so why should her needs matter. Anyway, it's all in your mind. Just don't let her see what you really look like—a shapeless cloud of energy. I suggest you assume a form that has more…definition."

That urging was all Ra needed. He eyed the temp, swallowed his pride, lowered his energy vibes to match hers, reached out with his mind…and touched her.

The look on her face was priceless. Had she been working in another spot; she might have stayed hidden until he walked away. But she didn't.

At first, she scanned him with hungry eyes, even furrowed her brow and hesitantly thought, *When did you come in?*

Then, upon closer inspection, she found herself regarding him as breathtakingly handsome.

She shook her head and wondered, *Why do males like you keep walking into my life?* Yet, she welcomed the intrusion into her otherwise boring existence. The carefully rehearsed company greeting script was quickly forgotten, replaced with one of her own.

Well over six feet tall. Creamy, golden—brown luminous skin touched by a glint of lavender blue, slightly lighter than the rich layers of bright violet hues that comprised his energy field. Dripping with attitude. He made something inside her leap as she recalled the tingle that accompanied the thought of burning desire, raised the possibly that she could forget the pain and loneliness carefully hidden among the other ruins of her existence. Suddenly, she wanted to get to know this stranger. She wanted him to find her. Keep her safe.

He was a stranger. That excited her, sweetened the thought of a mental escapade with him. *You might be in your mid-to-late twenties or a great deal older. I really don't care. Whatever your age, you're just right for me. I want you to want me. Show it. Mean it.*

The unruly strand of hair had once again come loose. Instead of smoothing it back in place, she toyed with it, wrapped it around her fingers as her mind phased to a preoccupation that she often took refuge in—daydreaming.

Never taking time to cultivate her own natural beauty, she relied on a quick fix of makeup to create the mask the company required her to show. But in her daydreams, she could take off the mask, reveal herself any way she wanted, do anything she wanted. With no regrets.

In her mind, she saw herself in two places at the same time—the office, but also floating in some secret corner of the Realm, serenaded by mellifluous sweet tones that swirled and spiraled while she snuggled between the bright violet and lavender blue layers of his energy field…his vibe.

In that magical place, he would move to undress her. Not wanting to give him the impression she was easy, she would refuse his advances. Romance…then surrender.

She sank deeper and deeper within her dream, enough to imagine a starlight canopy that cradled them as he pulled her towards him and embraced her. Warm kisses as her mouth found and gently sucked his full and pouty lower lip. Playful tickles turned into craving need. The tender caress of his hands as they wandered over her essence, found then lingered in sensitive zones she never imagined. Her skirt, then her blouse, then every…hesitation abandoned until she no longer protested when he exposed and explored what she had so carefully hidden, then pledged himself to her as their vibes united in one passionate climax.

Too bad it could only happen in her imagination.

Calm your waves, she blushed. *Who am I kidding. What can I possibly have to offer someone like him? We're strangers. Besides, he might be…one of them. Don't send vibes that advertise a desire for something more than a superficial, professional conversation.* Then again, the thought of her face brushing against his coarse black chest hair charged different parts of her own ethereal body and caused her arms, hands, feet, every aspect of her soft yellow layers to fill with swirls of shimmering rose hues.

Embarrassed by her own boldness, she prayed that he wouldn't notice. She ran her tongue across her own lips, formed in the perfect shape of a cupid's bow, only to discover that she'd forgotten to apply ChapStick under her lipstick. Dry and tight as they had become, she shuddered to imagine what the remnants of her signature ruby red lipstick must look like.

Just my luck, she thought, as her tongue found embarrassing cracks, tiny pieces of flaking skin, and little dry spots.

Chapter 5

From somewhere deep inside Ra's essence, a warning sounded to proceed with caution. Silky smooth like black velvet, the baritone voice wasn't his. And it certainly wasn't like the low, deep, raspy voice that plagued him. This one was distinctive…and peaceful.

As if the speaker knew Ra, it cautioned, "Don't get distracted."

But he paid it no mind. He was used to getting caught-up in self-destructive ego trips and rarely obeyed such harbingers of the obvious.

Ra studied the temp and thought, *She's actually eyeing me and licking her lips!*

"Not quite the kind of professional behavior one would expect." The comment from the low, deep, raspy voice was matter-of-fact. "Maybe they make an exception for her. I wonder if she's having an affair with the boss? Picture yourself catching a glimpse of her with him; or, better still, almost getting caught with her yourself in some secluded supply room in the middle of a compromising act, like those your elders say could never really happen in Sun City. Yeah, wouldn't that make you feel happy? It might even make the thought of pursuing her worth the risk."

Pushing…urging Ra to go farther away from the wisdom offered by the deep voice that was so peaceful and distinctive. Keeping the pressure on until a sudden rush of red intensified the richness of his bright violet layers, turning them from violet to deep purple. Finally the rebel in him gave in. Ra's gaze met hers, held it for more than a few seconds as he played mind games…unexplored selfish desires and imagined lustful gratification…pulled her into a fantasy he created…into his vibe.

The thought of an encounter in a supply room intrigued him. In his mind's eye, Ra pictured such a room nestled in a corner of a seldom used hallway. No bigger than a small closet, it would be dimly lit by one naked lightbulb that dangled at the end of a cord suspended from the ceiling that could be tuned on and off from a wall switch. Dusty and seldom used, provisions would be kept there—paper, pencils and so on—all neatly stacked in piles on top a table sturdy enough to bear a heavy weight load. He would guide her essence into that space, send supplies flying as he eased her back on that table top, undid her blouse, fondled her breasts, kissed her lips as her fingertips traced paths through his jet-black coils, ran up and down his neck in route to the curly hairs of his full and wide beard, shaped into a perfect curve at his cheeks and square jawline. Her fingertips would tingle with warmth as she slowly unbuttoned his fitted shirt, combed their way through the mat of coarse black hair that covered his chest. A wave of tension would pulse through her essence, then melt, only to happen again…and again. And, when she unzipped his pants…

His mind tired of the effort as the initial excitement faded. Just like that, he mercifully dropped his gaze, released her. His emerald green eyes sparkled in amused satisfaction at her dumfounded expression. *Yes,* he vowed. *that's what I'd do, if only I could and as long as I got my kicks.*

As if on cue, the low, deep, raspy voice observed, "You're doing fine, Ra. You're doing fine."

Mercy, what's happening to me? Not yet free of Ra's intrusion, waves of deep red crimson washed over the temp's layers, almost totally obscured the soft yellow glow of her own energy field.

It wasn't like her to dwell on such topics. She knew it was impossible, but still blushed at the thought of how it would be to actually explore his athletic physique in a comfortable, intimate setting.

Embarrassed, the temp looked at Ra with a kind of wide-eyed innocence, suddenly unable to remember the reason he stood there. She inhaled deeply, slowly released the breath and murmured, "Check in, sir?"

"I have an appointment for the job opening."

"Which one? What time?"

" Creator God Apprentice, and right about now."

The sound of his baritone voice was deep, resonant, and incredibly gorgeous.

"I sent my application form in last week."

"Your name, please."

"Ra."

Surprised by his brevity, she hesitated, then inquired, "Is Ra your first or last name?"

"That's all there is. Just Ra."

Keenly aware that her time with him was about to come to an end, she begrudgingly mumbled, "All right," then pointed to her left and added, "The waiting area is over there. He probably already knows you're here and will be with you shortly."

"Thank you."

The temp watched as Ra made his way to the designated waiting area, then began a search for his application. The small oaken desk she sat at was an antique. It only had three storage drawers, all locked with the exception of the one at the bottom labeled Job Applicant Forms, Returned, Ready for Processing. She pulled it open and was surprised to find it was empty. *I wonder if his application might be one of those on the floor behind the desk, one I haven't come to yet.*

The frantic search which followed confirmed her suspicion. She quickly typed his name on a label and stuck it on a blank folder, retrieved his paperwork from the jumble on the floor, and made sure his application form was safely inserted. All done efficiently, she had time left over to observe him from behind…, admire the way his pants clung to his perfectly shaped butt and how he moved with a swagger of his shoulders.

She smiled and licked her lips. *He looks as good going as coming.*

Chapter 6

It was the job of the front desk receptionist to know which telephone line connected to which office. That way the company could avoid mix-ups which might prove…embarrassing.

The usual process called for the receptionist to push the appropriate button to alert the appropriate office that a visitor had arrived.

Except in the case of the office at the end of the long hallway on the right. That button would light-up on its own, almost as an afterthought.

Now was one of those times when the button flashed red on its own, just as Ra walked away from her desk and before she touched it…like the caller was already informed of his presence. When the telephone rang, she reached out, gripped the receiver, then raised it to her ear. Her face paled and her smile dissolved into wide-eyed panic as she listened to the voice of the speaker on the other end of the line.

Just as he was getting settled, Ra felt the faint pressure of an energy field nervously bump up against him.

"Follow me, please." It was the temp, standing there, holding a folder with what looked like his name typed on it.

But her tone of voice was different, strained, almost as though she was choking.

Her ethereal body hovered close to him. This time minus the telltale shimmering rose swirls, the layers of her trademark soft yellow energy field were pulled close around her as though she didn't want to be noticed. She took steps that were short and hurried as they crossed to the other side of the space and proceeded along the long narrow hallway.

We usually just tell them where to go. Why am I being directed to act as a personal escort for this deity? Have I done something wrong? Am I the one being evaluated?

They passed office spaces with closed doors of every size and made from every type of material until they came to a plain door made of weathered pine. It was the door at the end of the hallway. Unpretentious and unlabeled, it echoed the rough texture and rust feel of wood: ancient, perhaps as old as time itself.

From where she stood in the hallway, the temp heard voices slightly muffled against the closed door, engaged in a heated debate.

She knocked one time, softly. No response.

Why don't you answer? she wondered. *I know you're in there. I can hear you.*

Her shoulders rounded into a slouched position as an invasion of gray filaments quickly turned her soft yellow bloom into a dingy echo of its joyful glory.

Ra and the temp stood close…too close to each other. He saw what was happening. It wasn't that she meant anything to him; it was the sudden change in her vibes that interested him. Before he could move away, boundaries were crossed. What he dreaded most happened. Infiltration. A portal opened between them and he experienced her reality.

The rich, bright violet and lavender blue layers of his own energy field became dingy and a little gray. His muscles tightened. His stomach churned. It was hard to breathe. Unsure what to do, he stood there in silent agony. He had no name for it, but elders in his colony had spoken of a time in the distant past before the cleansing, about something called feelings and emotions.

There was one they whispered about in particular. They called it fear.

He wondered, *could this be fear? What is she afraid of?*

Chapter 7

The temp nervously shifted her weight from one foot to the other, then drew in a deep breath and exhaled. She knocked again, this time more sharply. Still no response.

Panicked, she wondered, *what should I do?* From somewhere deep inside of her essence came a whisper. "Knock again." Smooth as black velvet, the baritone voice was so soft and kind. *Is that you, my faithful encourager?*

Just as she raised her hand to knock, a different male voice, deep and authoritative, barked an order from somewhere on the other side of the door.

"Enter."

She hesitated for a second, then reached for the tarnished metal handle, turned it, gave it a nudge, ever so slightly. The door creaked on well-worn hinges. It held firm as it swung inward but only so far. Some obstacle kept it from opening all the way.

Never having imagined such an invitation as possible, the temp was unsure about what her next move should be. *Stand in the hallway and let this deity pass alone into the room? Make the first move into the office, announce him, then wait patiently until dismissed?*

No one, especially at her low level, really knew what happened behind that door. Buzz words like "power broker pacts" and "high stakes deals"…conjecture, nothing more than food for the muted conversation of the office gossip mill. She decided to play it safe, offer a certain degree of cautious respect. She didn't care or want to be involved; yet there she was, standing in the hallway in front of that door, being directed to enter.

Hoping that her ordeal was soon coming to an end, the temp gathered what passed for courage. With head bowed and gaze lowered, she stepped across the threshold and mumbled, "Excuse me, sir, but this deity, Ra, has an appointment with you."

Ra could hardly hear her, but from where he stood in the hallway, and with the door partially open, he could see most of the space inside the office.

Sparsely furnished, there was a plain wooden desk and two chairs. Both chairs were positioned behind the desk, close to each other.

One was a straight-backed wooden chair. Large, with armrests, it was partially nestled into the well of the desk and occupied by a deity, one who was definitely masculine.

The other chair was off to the right. Seemingly unoccupied, it was quite different than the one the deity sat in. Austere and high backed, it virtually oozed charm and character. Made of oak, it was heavily carved with elaborate ribbons and floral designs on scrolled arms and long cabriole legs. The small, luxurious velvet pillow that rested on top of its cane seat more than guaranteed a comfortable experience.

The walls were bare, with the exception of a framed painting of a perfectly symmetrical ostrich feather, brownish gray in color, with the hollow shaft pointed downward. A work of art, the frame had a vintage look to it and was gold in color. It hung on the wall immediately behind the desk.

Ra's gaze shifted back to the deity and he marveled at what he saw. *He's dressed with a stylish flair that befits a being of his station. His suit is tailored, charcoal black, six button double-breasted with a long-sleeved white shirt, black silk tie, and gold cufflinks. I wonder if his shoes are brand new? Black pumps…the fancy kind, detailed with a polished shine. Those dark blood-red eyes. They seem to peek out from beneath his bushy gray-flecked eyebrows, the same color as the hairs of the curly thick mustache that hangs just above his trimmed full beard.* Ra marveled at his appearance. He chuckled to himself and thought, *This deity is completely bald so he must be ancient, but his skin is burnished to a lustrous finish…the color of copper, deep rose gold mixed with brown. From here it looks almost flawless, as smooth as diamond crystals, untouched and deep within the gray heart of the Heavenly Realm.*

Chapter 8

The deity sat behind his desk, one leg crossed over the other, his fingers folded in a steeple position. He regarded both Ra and the *temp* thoughtfully. *How much did they hear?* He had to know, get to know, both of them.

First, the temp. He studied her thoughtfully then concluded, *There's fear in your vibe. I need to get you to trust me.*

His full lips curved into a broad smile, and he immediately worked the magic he was so well known for. He turned on the charisma and murmured, "Thank you…Lynette is it?" then observed her reaction.

Bubbles of soft yellow and splashes of glittery pink flooded her energy field.

For a second, just below fake translucent glowing layers of gold, his true murky brown splashed with muddy yellow-green hues boiled and flashed, swirled in and out, went round and round. The deity strained to stifle a scornful laugh and thought, *There's power in a name. Does it make you feel special to hear me say yours?*

The *temp* raised her gaze and replied, "Yes sir."

"Well, Lynette. You haven't been here for one full day. But I've heard about the fine job you're doing handling that front office assignment. An exemplary greeter. Efficient, organized, focused. This place would benefit by having more employees work as hard as you. I occasionally review employee background checks. You are a third plane deity?"

"Yes, sir."

"Well, you're much too good a worker to be stuck at this Field Office in such a low-level position. You belong at my Headquarters in a better area on the West side. You'd be with a higher level staff and have security clearance. Keep it up, and I have no doubt you'll soon be considered for a permanent position, perhaps administrative. I'll give it some thought. We'll discuss it tomorrow."

His voice, so deep and authoritative. And he knows my name. The temp forgot all about ChapStick and lipstick and dry, tight lips. For the first time in a very long time, she began to feel…valued.

The Court—a new beginning! A place where I'll be protected and *appreciated.* The flattery. The acknowledgement. It made her essence pulse with waves of joy. A smile flickered across her face that rivaled the brilliance of a small nova. She stood erect and seemed more at ease. And her energy field…not a gray filament to be seen in any of her layers; only glowing bubbles of luminous yellow light and splashes of glittery pink with light baby blue hues, reflections of gratitude and confidence.

She placed the folder on his desk then backed out of the office. Her positive mind-set revived, she wondered, *perhaps everything that happened to me was a blessing in disguise. No matter now. I'm once again a face with a name. I claim my name…Lynette. Maybe I'll sign-up for that administrative training course and get a bona fide certificate.*

Lynette. The change in her vibes pleased Ra. He smiled, aware of how he suddenly wanted to say her name, over and over again. Somehow knowing her name made the thought of her more than just a toy to be used for his pleasure. That intrigued him, made him wonder about…possibilities.

The open doorway wasn't large enough to accommodate them both at the same time. When Ra stepped aside to let Lynette move into the hallway, her new vibe touched him and restored his energy field to its vibrant glory. Grateful for the relief, it bothered him that she brushed past without so much as a word or gesture of recognition. *I wanted to compliment you on how that ray of bright white light emanating from the center of your essence gives your layers an airy, feminine quality.* His emerald green, almond-shaped eyes sparkled as he wondered, *Why didn't I notice that radiant light before? Perhaps I've been too hasty, misjudged you…would have wronged you. Service to others. That must be your true calling. An assignment at The Court will improve your work status. Perhaps we'll meet again. I wonder what you would do if I revealed my true self to you?*

With a slight upward turn to his full lips, he smiled.

Chapter 9

Ra had always worked at one thing or another, but just hadn't found his niche, the job that was right for him. Now he was interviewing for the top management position in Sun City, directly under the supervision of the highest deity in the Heavenly Realm.

This was a rare opportunity, indeed. As a rule, he didn't enjoy interviews, didn't like the idea of humbling himself before anyone. *It's all about their vibes. They never really want to know who I am or what I believe.*

"Just play the game. Things will be different this time." The low, deep, raspy voice was back in his head, this time crystal clear and filled with arrogance. "The stakes are high as they can get. Land a job that's worthy of you and in the process impress your elders."

Ra thought about how the deity received Lynette, how he spoke with warmth and kindness. The lavender blue and bright violet hues of his energy field sparkled as he quietly resolved that, when his time came, he would remain calm and confident. *Now I understand why Lias encouraged me to apply for this position. What better role model could there be than the* Great Creator God himself. *What an honor to witness firsthand all the noble acts I know he will perform.*

That's exactly what he told himself as he stood in the hallway facing the deity.

It would prove to be a terrible misjudgment of character.

This time, the tone of voice that came from the other side of the open door was almost formal. It broke Ra out of his reverie.

"Come in please and close the door."

The deity was content to stay out of the spotlight. He valued his privacy. On those rare occasions when he left the building, he purposefully kept a low profile.

After all, who could he trust?

Even though he had a lot on his mind, Ra had been on his radar from the first moment he saw him standing in the hallway. Now that Lynette was out of the way, his attention turned to him.

A keen observer of behavior, he studied the way Ra moved, spoke, his posture, and most of all the lavender blue and bright violet hues that comprised the layers of his energy field. *He's young, probably just a sprite. No matter, there is something about him. Yes, could he be the one judged more worthy than myself? I'll test his mettle. Words might lie, but vibes always speak the truth.*

Just as Ra turned around to close the door, the profile of an object resting behind it caught his eye. It was what kept the door from opening all the way.

Another straight-backed wooden chair, armless, with a cane seat.

The deity watched him without speaking, then said, "As you know, this is a Field Office. It's a step-down from Headquarters. Convenient when necessary. I try to make sure it has all the comforts of…home."

He pointed to the armless chair, then to a spot facing the desk and made a request. "Ra, would you mind bringing that chair over here?"

"Yes sir," he said, but thought, *I didn't come here to be your servant,* and hoped the lopsided smile that made its way across his full lips wouldn't betray him.

Ra casually strolled over to the chair and picked it up. *How heavy it is,* he thought. *I'm surprised it isn't lighter.*

Still seated in his cross-legged position, the deity continued watching. "That's right. Bring it over here. Now have a seat, and make yourself comfortable."

"Yes, sir. Thank you, sir." Ra did as directed, then settled down on the hard seat and waited.

Chapter 10

Few had enough nerve to come before the deity for any reason, let alone to compete for a coveted position. Of those who did, only one had been a serious contender. But, in the end, he wasn't "the one" the deity was looking for.

The position of Creator God Apprentice was one step below his own and came with the title of Lord, an elevation above all other deities, not to mention access to certain classified information. There might come a time when he needed an ally. If that happened, he and his apprentice needed to be of one mind. And if something happened to him, he needed to know that his apprentice would continue his agenda, his vibe. That's why the interview process was taken seriously, even staged with an uncomfortable chair and controversial questions.

The deity scooted his chair closer to his desk, then propped his head up on one arm and studied Ra in silence. What seemed like an eternity was actually only a few seconds. He picked up the folder, opened it and briefly scanned the completed application. Then he lifted his gaze to Ra. His blood-red orbs flashed with a curious glow. He began a line of questioning designed to see how far he could push Ra before he buckled under pressure.

"I've reviewed your application. You haven't had any practical experience even close to the job you're applying for."

Blushes of bright yellow retreated as faint pulses of gray washed over colors and hues that defined Ra's magnificent layers. His eyes opened wide as he gazed at the deity, shrugged his shoulders and mumbled, "The notice said experience wasn't necessary."

A forced half-smile was followed by a frown as the deity replied, "Uh, true, so it did." The smooth, copper-toned skin that defined the deity's wrinkled forehead fractured into a web of little wrinkles as his thoughts drifted back to the particulars spelled-out in the notice. His unblinking gaze bored deep into Ra's emerald green eyes, the trademark color possessed only by second plane deities, and wondered, *did you miss the part about "only second plane full status deities need apply?"*

"Well tell me, what skills and strengths can you bring to this position?"

Ra hesitated for a second, then quipped, "I like to describe myself as charismatic, even persuasive. The decisions I make are amazingly correct. I'm ambitions and usually get what I go after."

The wry smile that floated across one side of the deity's full lips exposed the tips of perfect white teeth. His gaze remained steadfast as he chuckled softly and scoffed, "Quite the extrovert. You probably do well at social gatherings."

Ra's body tensed as his cocksure bravado started to wither under the poker-faced stare of the deity's blood-red orbs.

Chapter 11

With every second that passed, the pupils of the deity's blood-red orbs contracted more and more, intensifying his cold stare as he probed further.

"That tells me something about your personality. But I'm more interested in your character. After all, it's not every day that a run-of-the-mill deity gets an opportunity to be considered for a job like Creator God Apprentice."

Inexperienced, perhaps. But Ra had never been referred to as "every day" or "run-of-the-mill."

Ra's shoulders tensed. The game had gone too far for him to openly admit he was actually masquerading as inferior for his own purpose. Caught in the middle, he was exactly where the deity wanted him to be.

Like quicksilver, the interview took an even more curious turn. The deity lowered his gaze for a second, then raised it as he turned to face a golden translucent mist, lighter than fog and tinged with swirls of pure white and rich purple. It had suddenly settled on the velvet pillow on the seat of the austere, high-backed oaken chair to his right.

Cocooned within the translucent mist, the outline of a shape slowly took form. Male, it gave off a vibe that was undeniably positive. The exchange that took place between them caused muddy yellow and forest green with dull gray splashes to peak out from under his contrived layers of gold.

Following a short interval, the deity turned back to face Ra. He drummed his fingers on the desk top, then leaned forward toward Ra and said, "Let me be blunt. What makes you think you're qualified? I mean, Creator God Apprentice…learning to create universes and realities. That's a high level of responsibility, one that calls for honesty and integrity."

Chapter 12

Ra's emerald green eyes shifted nervously from left to right. His face paled as he realized that his deception had been discovered. *Now this deity is playing games with me, using me for his amusement.*

His strategy had backfired, and he had no choice but to endure the humiliation. He took the deity's comments as put-downs, and it completely deflated his confident posture. In that instant, he realized the impact of the mental games he so casually played with others. Now that it was happening to him, the thrill of the game was gone. He sat in stunned silence. His breath quickened as he thought, *The deity knows I am not what I pretend to be.* It took all his resolve to keep black waves, dark as night shadow, from overtaking the splendor of his colors and hues. For some reason, his thoughts turned to Lynette, and he was thankful that he couldn't act on what he dreamed for her.

Before continuing, he flashed an anxious smile at the deity and mumbled, "I'm sorry. I don't quite understand what you're asking."

"I think you do," the deity replied. "Would you say that you are honest and truthful?"

Ra sensed muddy, yellow-green hues start to wash throughout his own magnificent energy field. He lowered his gaze and cringed at the prospect of being exposed as a liar, not to mention the consequences of being disqualified from the applicant pool. He nervously picked at a loose piece of wood on the arm of his chair until it broke-off into a long splinter.

He had nothing left to lose.

In desperation, a silent sigh escaped from between his full lips. *Where do I go from here?* Again, he heard a baritone voice as smooth as black velvet come from somewhere deep inside his essence. Never demanding, it whispered, "There's only one thing you can do. Humble yourself. Tell the truth."

When he finally raised his gaze, the face he showed to the deity was clouded with regret. For the first time in his very short existence, Ra fought back tears that pooled in his emerald green, almond-shaped eyes.

"Sir, I have a confession to make. I don't have full status as a second plane deity."

The deity leaned back in his chair. He ran his fingers through the curly hairs of his thick salt-and-pepper mustache, being careful not to go so deep as to scratch the tender skin above his upper lip. He regarded Ra with a gaze that seemed to search the depths of his very essence, breathed a deep sigh and said, "Don't you think I know that? Why didn't you just tell the truth?"

A dazed look of bewilderment raced across Ra's face. He stared at the deity sheepishly as he gripped the arms of the chair. "All I know is that Lias, eldest deity of all second plane colonies, thought my credentials were strong enough to apply for the position right now, even though the coming-of-age ritual is still months away. Evidently, he thinks there is some additional honor I might qualify for if I go to that ritual having already performed a noble act. Working for you would give me that opportunity."

The deity gazed at Ra, then turned, faced the mist in the chair beside him and muttered something Ra couldn't quite make out. Pausing for a second, he turned back to face Ra and asked, "Lias…did you say Lias?"

"Yes, sir. He thinks very highly of you."

The deity cocked an eyebrow and asked, "Does he? Interesting. That's *very* interesting."

"But, sir…"

"Yes, what is it?"

"I beg your forgiveness. I didn't see the wrong in what I did. I meant no harm. As unworthy as I am, I was desperate to get this job. The way you treated Lynette. You were so nice to her, and I sensed how her vibes changed as a result. I wanted you to treat me like that. That's why I gave in to temptation. I wanted to impress you. Please give me a chance to redeem myself, at least in your eyes."

The deity rose and began to walk toward Ra with steps that were sure and steady. He edged closer and closer until he stood next to Ra, then reached toward him and placed his hands on his shoulders. He had a strong grip and despite being wrinkled with age spots, his hands had a rectangular shape with long, slender fingers and nails slightly yellowed, yet well-manicured. With a nonchalant confident expression, he bent forward to meet Ra's gaze. In a hoarse whisper, he mumbled, "Stand. Let me give you my blessing. Everyone deserves a second chance. We'll move forward from here."

The deity embraced Ra until he was totally enfolded within his own layers, then released him from his grip and pivoted on his heels to make his way back across the room. Instead of sitting in his chair, he stopped next to the desk and perched on one edge with his legs crossed, ankle over knee. Lost in thoughtful observation, he eyed Ra in an attempt to judge the impact of his declaration.

He was not disappointed.

Once again seated in the straight-backed wooden chair, Ra's energy field was streaked with ribbons of light blue and rose red.

"Ra, do you believe in loyalty?

"I like to think so."

"Are you a team player?"

"Well, I never had an opportunity to…"

"Would you compromise your personal values for the good of the whole, perhaps to keep the peace?"

"I…"

"And unconditional love? What are your thoughts regarding unconditional love?"

Ra considered the question. "I'm sorry. I don't know what that is."

The deity tilted his head to one side and said, "Do you love others despite their faults? Would you…" Seeing the puzzled expression of Ra's face caused the corners of the deity's mouth to lift into a smile and the smooth skin around his eyes to crack into little wrinkles.

"Oh, well, forget it," *for now*.

The deity stood up, turned and walked back to his chair behind the desk. Once there, he plopped down, then turned to face the translucent mist parked on the austere high-backed oaken chair off to his right.

Until that moment, the mist had remained dim and unchanging. Now its splendid layers were becoming brighter and more defined.

The deity reached out towards the light as if consulting it about something. It became brighter and pulsed, but never displayed as anything more than a shapeless cloud of translucent mist. After a few seconds, the deity smiled. He stroked and twisted the curly salt-and-pepper hairs of his beard between aged fingers with an amazing agility. Then, he turned toward Ra and continued the interview.

Chapter 13

A satisfied smile crossed the deity's lips as he considered all that had happened. *Temptation*, he wondered. *Could that be your weakness? I've discovered more than expected. The young and inexperienced are so easily manipulated. Yes, Lias and I know each other very well. So, now he thinks I perform noble acts? Lias takes his direction from The Almighty. I wonder what He's up to?* His thoughts shifted back to Ra. *Temptation, that will be your undoing. You will serve my vibes and after that…well, I don't care what happens to you. In fact, my blessing will turn into a curse. I'll give you a task and make sure you fail.*

"It's true that no prior experience is required. Everyone has to start somewhere."

The deity's blood-red orbs sparkled with amusement as he raised his bushy eyebrows in Ra's direction and said, "Except in my case. I was my own starting point. Am I not magnificent? Anyhow, what's important is where you finish. You do understand that any formal offer of employment will only be made after successful performance during your probationary period. Then there's the matter of your apprenticeship. I'll need to make sure you're a good fit for the position."

"Yes, sir, that is to be expected."

The deity hesitated, then said, "Now swear an oath of loyalty to me, and don't take it lightly. You see, there are forces working against me, lies being circulated that might tempt you to doubt my supremacy. I'll expect you to inform me of any unexpected revelations that come your way and treat all information as strictly confidential, just between the two of us, for the good of everyone involved. Understand?"

"I understand, Great Creator God. I swear to be loyal to you…only to you."

Once again, the deity regarded the shapeless cloud of translucent mist to his right, then turned to face Ra. A grin crossed his face that was almost from ear to ear.

"There's something about you that makes me hopeful. I'm going to give you a chance. I wonder…yes, I just might have something suitable. It will definitely be demanding, but anything you do from this point on, if done incorrectly, could have eternal repercussions.

"A situation has been brewing on one of the planets I, uh, created, eons ago. I called it Earth."

At the mention of Earth, the light resting on the austere high-backed chair grew dim, then flared up and blazed with an unexpected intensity.

With a wave of his hand, the deity continued. "That planet will be my gift to whoever completes the apprenticeship and moves on to bigger things. You know, to experiment with, use as a template for future endeavors. It won't matter because the creatures who live there, humans, are inferior to us. I need that situation resolved. That deity deserves to start with a clean slate, not with my unfinished business.

"Now, about those humans. Worthless creatures. I reached out, tried to show them exactly what the elders of your particular plane preach; the importance of discipline and control. I would satisfy all their wants and needs to give them more time to pursue loftier activities, like devising creative ways to worship me. The only thing I required was that live, grow, and thrive by my vibe, not theirs. Submit. That's all they had to do to show their gratitude.

"The mistake I made was to leave them unsupervised. Many made the wise decision to obey my commandment. Those who didn't caused problems, even to this day. Rabble-rousers. Agitators. All in one particular location. Now everything is out of balance. Thankless ingrates! I'm told they gather in secret places, scheme and plot to keep rebels from…conversion.

"I need answers. Why do they resist the gift I offer? Go down to Earth, be an observer, find out who their leader is. Report your findings back to me. Help me understand."

The deity gave a barely perceptible nod of his head. With both eyes half closed and just a little too calculating, he continued. "In fact, it might work to my—our—advantage that you're a second plane deity. Earth is a planet in the fourth plane. You seem to be good at playing games, so play the game of being human. Make them trust you. Find some way to get what I need. Do the job well, and when you come back, you'll move on to the next level."

The shadow of a sly grin passed across his full lips as the deity studied Ra with shrewd eyes. "How does Lord Ra sound? As my apprentice, I'll train you to carry on my work, be a conduit for my vibe in the event something happens to me. You'll become a resident of first plane. Of course, I'll give your performance a top-notch rating that will more than impress Lias."

Ra let out a long breath, then smiled and said, "I really appreciate this opportunity, sir. I won't disappoint you."

"I hope not."

"Sir, is that where I'll be stationed, on Earth?"

The deity shook his head. "Goodness, no. You're going to have enough to deal with without dwelling in that place. You'll be based here in Sun City, the capital of the Heavenly Realm. In fact, if I'm not mistaken, space is available at The Court on the West side. When you get there, you'll meet my…associate, Isfet. He'll be at your disposal. You can rely on him."

The deity's expression hardened as he thought, *Nothing must threaten the well-being of my reign, here in Sun City or on Earth.* His brows lifted as he continued, "By the way, there may also be a bit of housekeeping for you to do here in Sun City and…" A new thought crossed his mind, caused him to pause in mid-sentence, then add, "You're not the first to apply for this position. Many have come before you but were disqualified for one reason or another." His full lips curved into a knowing smile. "You might encounter at least one of them. You never know who might harbor hard feelings." He looked as if he might say something more on the topic, but cleared his throat and instead said, "You'll be on your own. I suggest you remain vigilant at all times."

Ra waited for more information, but none was given.

"I'm in and out of my office at The Court. If you really need me, I'll leave instructions with Lynette as to how you can contact me."

"Then she's going to move to The Court?"

"Oh, most definitely." *She's a looker all right. With her seated only a few feet from my office, it'll be easier to keep my eyes on her. And for more than one reason.*

From where he sat in his chair behind the desk, the deity watched Ra as he rose, turned and walked toward the door. He cocked his head and contemplated Ra's future with mixed emotions. *Desire-my favorite temptation.*

Just as he reached the door, Ra turned back to face the deity. He plucked at the cuffs of his shirt sleeves and asked, "By the way, sir, how should I address you?"

"I've been known by many names. You may call me by my given name, Karoon."

"And, when will the assignment start?"

"Today. You can go over there right now. Just continue along this street until you come to the very end. You can't miss it."

Chapter 14

Ra's happiness knew no bounds. Everything he envisioned was about to come true. And a shot at Lynette! It was all he could do to keep his energy field from exploding into a flurry of colors.

He followed the golden street to the highest point. The last building he came to was nestled within a secured space at the very end.

Excited and a little nervous, he stood in the courtyard. Designed to make a statement, there was only one caption on a huge red sign. Starlight Office Court was spelled out in huge block letters, alongside Karoon's signature logo: an image of a perfectly symmetrical ostrich feather, brownish gray in color, hollow shaft pointing downward.

He sighed and thought, *This must be the place.*

All ten stories were reserved for the exclusive use of Karoon, his dark worker minions, and a few light workers for appearance's sake. Ra tilted his head back and looked upward as he tried in vain to see the top of the ten-story building, partially hidden by layers of gray and patchy white clouds that floated in the dismal, dreary sky.

When he looked back, he could see the Field Office and warehouse in the distance. He remembered how the building glowed like a luminous citadel. *It's too bad that end of the street isn't in better condition,* he thought, then turned to let his gaze drift slowly down the front side of The Court facade. He marveled at splendor, the likes of which he had never witnessed.

The colors of the facade sparkled with crystal clear clarity. Every inch shimmered in light that appeared to be illuminated from somewhere within the building. Deep blue sapphire, fiery jasper, yellow agate, green emerald, black onyx, translucent red carnelian, greenish yellow chrysolite, pink beryl, amber topaz, orange jacinth, and red-rimmed amethyst.

The front double doors opened to reveal a brightly lit, modern lobby filled with garden spaces. Ra walked across the threshold, impressed by the lustrous grayish white color of the walls and maze of corridors with square door openings.

One of the corridors was blocked off with a sign that read, AUTHORIZED PERSONNEL ONLY. When he walked a little further, his attention was drawn to a deity that suddenly appeared in a nearby square door opening. As he got closer, Ra saw it was male. Hidden behind a tall potted plant, the figure sported a gold neck chain and was dressed in a tacky dark blue pinstripe suit that had obviously seen better days.

Blood-red eyes, small and restless. A light brown-skinned face, narrow, with a short-bridged nose. Deep brown locks, pulled together in a loose ponytail dangling below broad shoulders. All embedded within an energy field with deep, muddy red and pink layers mixed with gray hues. Ra studied the deity's energy field and read his vibes in no time flat. *You're a second planer, but why are your eyes blood-red? Are your vibes corrupted? That's not a good sign. I wonder if Karoon's warning was about you? Ah, there it is. I see it in your layers and hues...muddy yellow-green...deceit. I've got to be careful. I may be standing in the presence of the only other competitor for the job I wanted.*

Ra lifted his chin in a gesture of contempt while his mouth twisted into a humorless smile.

Always on the lookout for a hot scoop, it was Isfet.

Chapter 15

Isfet eyed the newcomer with interest. *Karoon informed me to expect a male deity from the second plane. Ra...something or other. He's on probation for the Creator God Apprenticeship position, the same one I thought I had in my own back pocket. Betrayed, and I won't forget it. What makes Ra so special? And why wasn't I told the particulars about what he'll be doing? Karoon did mention that Ra's assignment had something to do with planet Earth. I'll make it my business to be first in the receiving line.*

"Hello? Hello! Welcome to The Court. My name is Isfet. And, you must be Ra." Isfet's words came out in a croak. "I heard you were coming. Congratulations, you passed the interview hurdle. Now you're on your way. No candidate has ever gotten this far. What an accomplishment. I'm so glad to meet you. I'm here to assist you in any way possible, fulfill your every desire. Everyone around here knows me. I can get anything you want or need and—"

"Thanks. That's most generous of you."

Unsettled by the abrupt manner in which Ra interrupted his well-phrased monologue in mid-sentence, Isfet grew uncharacteristically silent. He stood there, swayed back and forth as though the floor was collapsing beneath him. *I tried to be careful. I wonder if he sensed anything in my energy field that revealed my true nature?*

"Can you tell me where my office is?"

"Well, yes, it's on the tenth floor. We'll take the elevator."

The corners of Ra's mouth turned upward in a little smile. *I'm not going to walk up ten flights of stairs.* He scoffed at Isfet and said, "Please lead the way to the elevator."

They walked in silence, Isfet's wobbly gait a few steps ahead of Ra's cool, relaxed strut. As they entered the elevator, Isfet was the first to speak.

"I'll assume you're aware of the situation here in Sun City?"

Ra shot him a sideways glance. "Not entirely. Just that Karoon is concerned."

Isfet's gaze dipped to the floor as he shifted from one foot to the other. *Hmmm, that's interesting. Concerned about what? Specifics, I want specifics.* His small, blood-red eyes grew wide as he probed for more information.

"And, you're here to…?"

Again, Ra's response was brief and evasive. "Do a bit of housekeeping."

"Oh."

The elevator doors opened onto a small bright corridor. Before Ra could step out, Isfet pushed past him and almost knocked him into a metal stand that held a large engraved placard that read: Headquarters, Commander in Chief, The Heavenly Realm.

What the…? Before Ra could finish his thought, he looked up to see Isfet coming to an abrupt stop mid-stride just inches away from a figure lounged against the wall. His jaw dropped, shoulders slumped, and small blood-red eyes grew wide as he thought, *Well, look who's here. The high and mighty one himself. You think you're so special with your golden energy field, tinged with white and purple hues. I suppose some would call it radiant, but mine is so much nicer. You don't scare me. Don't you have anything else to wear besides that black suit and jacket? And, button up the top two buttons on your white shirt. Your pectoral muscle may be well defined, but what makes you think anyone wants to see your chest, peppered with tufts of curly black hair. And the way you stand, with your don't-mess-with-me attitude, the fingers of your right hand stuffed into your pants pocket while your left arm hangs freely at your side and your feet placed together in a parallel stance.*

"Hello, Isfet. I see you've been busy. As usual." With a mumbled inaudible curse, Isfet stumbled and almost fell as he quickly made his way back to the open elevator doors.

Needless to say, the moment was awkward. As the elevator doors closed, Ra turned to face the male deity by the placard. He furrowed his brow and inquired, "What …"

A smile danced around the corners of the deity's full lips. He replied in a tone that was controlled, baritone, like quiet thunder and almost familiar, "Never mind Isfet. He's temperamental, to say the least. Welcome to The Court." He reached up with one hand and smoothed his hair. Snow white and cut short, it was styled in a spiral of deep waves that obediently coiled around his head. "My name is Tobias. Karoon notified me that you were coming. I'm at your disposal."

"But, Isfet said he was going to—"

Tobias chuckled and replied, "He would say that. Let's just call his understanding a glitch in communication."

Chapter 16

As was true for most tyrants, Karoon chose a few deities to serve on what he called his Inner Council. They acted as a sounding board for all matters related to the governing of Sun City.

The selection process was tough as Karoon disqualified many applicants for one reason or another.

Dark workers were always his first consideration. There was never a dull moment when they were around. But a lack of control and a tendency to disobey orders and act recklessly limited their selection for such a serious assignment.

Then there were the catchers, dark worker agents loyal to Karoon. Catchers were automatically rejected. There were so many of them in Sun City that Karoon couldn't even remember them all. Holding a high-profile appointment would compromise their identities. Sensitive to how hues presented, they secretly monitored the population, always on the lookout for abrupt or subtle changes in colors and hues that might signal discontent.

Once exposed, Karoon would find a way to handle the offender.

That left one category—light workers who didn't appear a threat to him or his policies. At least openly. While it might not be genuine, Karoon took advantage of their true cheerful natures. He never passed up an opportunity to remind them that membership on the Council came with a higher status in Sun City than the other light workers enjoyed, along with privileges that made their precarious existence tolerable.

No light worker tried harder to please Karoon than Tobias. At least, that's how it seemed.

From the first moment he arrived in Sun City, Tobias started building a reputation that afforded him a certain amount of respect amongst both light and dark workers.

All agreed that he was suited to be a voice on the Inner Council, especially concerning all matters related to light workers. Unlike the others, Tobias was gifted in certain ways. He seemed to know things before they happened, which brought him a certain notoriety among the other deities. As his reputation grew, he came to Karoon's attention. He quickly appointed Tobias as his personal agent. But of course, Tobias knew this was destined to happen. Popular as he was, Karoon saw him as useful and referred to him as his special deity during public gatherings, even when attended by dark workers who considered themselves more worthy.

One thing was for sure. Tobias was a complex multifaceted deity. There were many sides to his personality— some he kept hidden behind a carefully constructed mask, some he revealed. Creative, honest, calm and dependable under pressure, his was the only legitimate gold energy field in Sun City.

And it was tinged with white and purple hues.

His vision for Sun City was quite different than the one held by Karoon. Coming from a place of pure positive energy, it was strategically planned, along with clearly defined steps to accomplish it.

Outwardly, Tobias posed no threat to Karoon or his policies. However, being on the Council put him in a prime position to observe much of the disarray in the City, to understand the need for change but in a positive direction.

Tobias felt that no dark worker had the right to tell any light worker what to think or do. He understood that Karoon's restrictions were there to serve his vibes, not theirs. Those who thought they knew him agreed it would be fatal to mistake his mellow demeanor for weakness. Perhaps light workers were trusting, easy-going, and cheerful but lacking a fighting spirit—never!

A true visionary and an eternal optimist, that was Tobias. Karoon wasn't perfect, but Tobias wasn't ready to give up on him. Not quite yet. He bided his time, waited for an opportunity to present itself that would challenge Karoon to reconsider the error of his ways. Benevolent, always willing to forgive, he excused Karoon's behavior while in mixed company, sometimes crediting it to a possible troubled past.

In the end, Tobias prophesied there would be dire consequences for Karoon if he continued on his current path. He foresaw the day when light workers would banish him from Sun City, most likely forcibly. For the time being, he would be an observer, but also secretly work with those determined to put an end to Karoon's cruelty, and pray that in the meantime he wouldn't lead them into darkness.

Chapter 17

Tobias led the way until they almost reached the end of the corridor, then stopped in front of double glass doors with thick steel frames and brass handles. He opened one and stepped across the threshold into what looked like a small unoccupied room that could have easily passed for a reception area.

Ra followed closely behind.

Eggshell white in color, the walls were seamless, with the exception of one that was paneled.

Tobias never broke his stride until he reached the paneled wall. Once there, he stopped, reached out and pushed a partially concealed button behind one of the panels. Part of the wall slid back to reveal a huge hidden office suite.

A wall of floor to ceiling windows framed unparalleled views of the Karoonsville skyline bathed in its usual dismal splendor.

The area was dominated by a huge executive desk, the kind with felt-lined drawers and raised panel detailing, with a woodsy brown finish and warm burgundy highlights. A leather-upholstered chair was nestled within the well of the desk.

A nearby credenza desk served as a second work station. Embedded within a hutch, it contained several lateral hanging files.

Two mahogany wood leather wingback chairs faced the desk. Situated along the far wall of the office were eight armless mesh chairs, fitted around a long rectangular, veneer custom conference table.

Tobias had been standing there, silent, observant, doing his best to pick up on anything that would serve as proof of Ra's character. He watched as Ra's eyes grew large and thought, *Lias was right about you. Your character does need a bit of tempering before you can step into the power I gave you and claim it. Look down, sprite. You're still on probation. The marble floor beneath your feet has a perfectly symmetrical ostrich feather, brownish gray in color, hollow shaft pointing downward emblazoned on it.*

Tobias pointed to a smaller closed door, wooden and unremarkable. It was located across the room in a corner of the wall behind the conference table. He hesitated for a second, then said, "Your office is through that door."

He watched how Ra took the news that was not to be his office space. The bright violet and lavender hues of Ra's energy field became increasingly flecked with patches of greenish-gray. Compassionate as Tobias was, that transition pulled at his heart strings. He kept a blank expression on his face as he wondered, *Could that possibly be an emotional connection? Let's see how you handle it when you walk into the next room.*

As he walked ahead of Ra, Tobias reached in his jacket pocket for the door key card, then stopped abruptly.

The door was already slightly ajar.

That's supposed to be entry by secure card access only, he thought. When Tobias touched the door, it swung open with a gentle shove.

A single motion was all it took for Tobias to reach back with his right hand and block Ra from entering the room. In a hushed tone he whispered, "Wait here." He walked ahead of Ra and scanned the room for intruders.

Satisfied there was no threat, he moved to one side and motioned Ra to follow.

Ra stood in the doorway and surveyed his new work area. It was a corner workspace. A window that wrapped around two sides of the building offered a reduced yet decent view of the skyline. A neutral color palate accented with tan and gray was the perfect choice to showcase a free-standing brass and glass desk. An executive chair with a cheery finish rested in the well. A conference table that could easily seat six was pushed to one side next to a wall.

It wasn't as grand as the larger space, but it would do just fine. The corners of Ra's lips curved upwards. That, along with a barely perceptible nod of his head betrayed his attempt to remain stoic.

Tobias watched as the bright violet and lavender hues of Ra's energy field began to clear, return to their original glory.

Oh, yeah, you've got potential, he though, as a quiet smile played at the corners of his mouth, found its way into his violet eyes and made them dance with childlike satisfaction.

"I hope this will be satisfactory." As if that wasn't enough for Ra to digest, Tobias continued. "This is the only floor in the building with a terraced lounge, game room and cafe, all at the other end of this corridor."

Small details, strategically delivered.

Suddenly the expression on Tobias' face grew somber. "This is one of the few times you'll have access to Karoon's private office suite. You'll work independently, but also be close enough for him to keep an eye on you. Just so you're aware." Then, he pointed to a second wooden door. It was closed and on the other side of the small work space. "You'll come and go through that door. It exits directly back into the hallway."

Chapter 18

Tobias didn't seem particularly surprised when he turned around and came face to face with two male deities.

Perhaps there was something about his energy, the unconditional love he radiated. Whatever it was, they felt it when his vibes touched theirs, and the joy it brought them guaranteed that no matter what was going on, they usually weren't far from his side.

What appeared as a lapse in judgement was actually a carefully orchestrated maneuver on their part. The two stood at the threshold of Karoon's office suite, carefully monitoring the interaction between Tobias and Ra. Pleased to find no sign of hostility, they chose to make themselves known.

A quiet smile of recognition spread across Tobias' face. "These are my associates, Julian and DaValla."

"I hope we're not late." Deep. Male. Baritone. DaValla's words filled spaces between a string of rapid, heavy breaths. Confident. Genuine. Well-balanced. Understanding. The eldest of Tobias' comrades, he was the one who tied them all together, their stabilizing force, their heart.

The only reason Tobias' pulse raced and his face paled was because of where DaValla stood. He didn't want to embarrass himself in front of Ra by showing how miffed he was, so his words came out in a controlled, sing-song cadence. "DaValla, you're not supposed to be in there. You're supposed to use the hallway entrance. Come on in."

"Wow! What a joint!" It was Julian, the youngest of the three. His high baritone voice had a deliciously golden quality not unlike his unrestrained and impetuous nature. Muscular as he was, Tobias considered him to be the brawn of the group.

Any pretense of annoyance in Tobias' voice was quickly extinguished by a deep sigh. His violet eyes softened to a prideful glow as his heart swelled with affection. "No, you're actually right on time," he murmured. As an afterthought, he inquired, "Did anyone see you on your way up here?"

Julian was the first to respond. "Funny you should ask that. We ran into Isfet in the lobby. He was getting out of the elevator. Just exchanged pleasantries, nothing more. Strange. He watched us until the elevator door closed, and the expression on his face wasn't friendly. More like, *what the hell are you up to?*"

Of all the bad luck. Tobias stood there, his brows furrowed in exasperation.

Julian's words registered somewhere in the back of his mind and for a second, Tobias lost his chain of thought. "Uhh, what did you say? Oh, yes, it was about Isfet." He waived his hand with a dismissive gesture.

In the meantime, handshakes were eagerly passed around.

As if he sensed something he couldn't quite put his finger on, DaValla addressed Ra in a tone that was profoundly reverent and sincere. "Sir, this is certainly an honor."

Tobias studied the lavender blue and bright violet hues that comprised the layers of Ra's energy field. When he saw no change in appearance, he said, "I hope you don't mind, but I asked them to meet us here."

"Not at all."

Tobias closed the door and motioned for everyone to take a seat at the small conference table in Ra's work space.

"I don't think we'll be disturbed in here." Just in case, he lowered his voice to almost a whisper as he turned to face Ra and inquired, "Did Karoon mention anything about housekeeping problems here in Sun City or on planet Earth?

"What an understatement!" DaValla's deep, booming baritone laughter warmed the room.

Tobias's companions always considered DaValla to be the brain of their little group. So they were perfectly comfortable letting him lead the conversation. His tone became somber as he leaned forward, studied Ra, and said, "I'll start with home base first. Something has gone terribly wrong here in Sun City. Thoughts of revolution are everywhere. We're divided into two groups, dark workers and light workers. Karoon's not concerned about his minions. Light workers have his full attention. Some of us have managed to keep our involvement in certain activities hidden. Karoon is suspicious. He's looking for a way to expose us, then control us."

"I don't know much about what's gone on in the City," replied Ra. "Deities in colonies on my plane live a rather sheltered existence. We tend to keep to ourselves. This is really the first time I'm hearing about outside affairs."

Tobias' gaze wandered first to DaValla, then to Julian. Their eyes riveted on him, heads nodded in agreement and urged him to continue.

Chapter 19

"Then I'll start from the beginning."

A wave of nostalgia swept over Tobias that caused his violet eyes to cloud with tears. He looked at Ra and said, "You'll never experience Sun City as I'm told it once was. Defined by a flurry of movement. Interaction. Separation. Slow. Quick. Pulse. Steady. Swirl. Bounce. Flicker. Blaze. A staggering amount of energy combined in every conceivable color and shade. Fine particulate layers of energy stored in etheric form, able to perceive and completely attuned to their own needs and the needs of others.

"In the beginning they were all light workers, reflections of feelings and emotions within layers of pure, positive energy. There were Singularities, loner ethereal deities who could merge with each other for a while, then separate and go their own ways as independent aspects; and Soul-mates, vibes of the same frequencies, always from the same plane who worked together in pairs.

"I'm told they gathered each morning in a section of the City called Aaru. While they could take any shape desired, each deity was an aspect of their true creator, *The Almighty*.

The greatest Creator God of all time. No one ever saw him, but they felt his presence in all the beauty and good that surrounded them. He gave them free will, allowed them self-determination. The choice each made was to be there and in return for their devotion there were no worries, nothing to stress them. Joy, harmony, peace, and nonviolence.

"A spirit of collaboration. Then one morning they awoke to find a peculiar mist snaking through the space they called home. Muddy yellow and forest green with splashes of dull gray, the fetid odor and clammy feel of it slithered down sidewalks and streets, engulfed courtyards and plazas, penetrated villas and work spaces. It reached Aaru, and as the mist became more translucent, a lone figure emerged, followed by hordes of twisted, gremlin-like deities with peculiar energy fields and menacing, blood-red orbs."

Tobias' violet orbs narrowed almost to slits as he continued.

"Karoon and his minions. Dark workers. Ethereal dimensional beings, purveyors of injustice, violence, and chaos. There was a time when they were decent enough, even compassionate and generous, or so I'm told. They went about their business, happy to scrape together a subsistence existence in the NoWhere very close to the border of the seventh plane."

DaValla had been carefully observing Ra. The questioning look he saw surprised him and caused him to interrupt Tobias to give further explanation. "Other than the seven planes, there is only the NoWhere—a chaotic place to be avoided at all costs."

"Thank you," replied Ra.

Tobias continued. "Karoon's influence changed them into the vain, selfish, emotionally detached beings who accompanied him that day. Whatever he did to them caused a complete disconnect from their own and other's emotions. Knowing that they were doing wrong to others no longer bothered them. The sign of their loyalty to him was an ostrich feather tattoo on their right forearms with the shaft pointing downward."

"Couldn't the light workers sense the evil in their midst?" Ra asked, his emerald green eyes wide with curiosity.

"That's possibly why Karoon picked Sun City. Light workers had no knowledge of evil. That is, until Karoon's arrival."

"Then why didn't *The Almighty* step in at that point and stop Karoon?"

"I'm not sure. But I'm told their plight caused *The Almighty* to weep. Perhaps he wanted to test them in some way, see if they would retain their peaceful nature or take on the ways of the invaders. Anyhow, once they realized the nature of their predicament, it was too late. They tried to protect themselves and what followed was a horrific battle, a clash of vibes. A blinding blitz of colors and hues. Bright yellow, pink, orange and light red, muddy forest green, dull gray, pulsing and flashing to a cacophony of buzzing crackles, pops and rumbles.

The prospect of immortality in the absence of the truth of all that defined them did not appeal to the light workers. The dark workers outnumbered them, but they fought to preserve all they had worked for. It seemed like the conflict would never end until one day Karoon stood in Aaru, the place where the sun rose, and approached them with a final solution. He proclaimed light and dark workers interdependent aspects of energy. It would be better for the City if they found a way to work together. Co-exist. Not wanting to risk the destruction of all they created, the light workers surrendered. Reluctantly, they acknowledged him as absolute ruler and he took over.

Karoon was a master military strategist. He waged other campaigns, but vowed this one would be his greatest. He was so focused on his goal that he failed to realize the light workers planned a strategy of their own. The world they loved was forever changed. While they might surrender their City, they vowed to never let Karoon touch who they truly were inside.

That's what they believed. But, it wasn't meant to be.

Time passed and Karoon's delusions of grandeur grew stronger. The light workers vowed to not betray their true natures. They would not become his minions. They would never thrive on the misery of others. That irritated Karoon, because it suggested his victory was not by a clear defeat. He didn't want to lose face before his followers, so he studied them. When he discovered their plan to deprive him of the glory and satisfaction he craved, he continued his efforts from a different angle.

By a stroke of luck, Karoon discovered that feelings and emotions were the things that defined light workers. That revelation pleased him. The experience with his minions gave him a false sense of confidence. He just needed to find the right approach to manipulate the light workers to get what he wanted. First, he re-defined their status as citizens of Sun City, tried to convince them they were lesser ethereal deities than either himself or his dark workers. That nearly caused a riot and made him realize it wasn't going to be as easy to subdue them as it had been with his minions. That's when he became desperate."

"Looks can be deceptive," muttered Julian.

Tobias nodded in agreement. "That's true. Before Karoon arrived, light workers put all their energy into managing their gifts, keeping them in check, using them to promote the greater good of the City, and so on. Following his arrival, their priorities changed. Frustrated. Powerless. Hopeless but still committed to fight on in any way they could."

"Karoon never anticipated that reaction," scoffed DaValla. "How ironic."

"Yes, it was," replied Tobias. "Karoon began to realize how easy it would be for them to use their resentment to spark a rebellion against him. Unless he found a way to suppress it. So, he tried a softer approach, told them something he thought might lull them into a false sense of security. He claimed they misunderstood him, that he was actually benevolent and only interested in their welfare. He claimed he knew how quickly the open and honest expression of feelings and emotions could get out of control, turn on them and become destructive. He created a law that forbid the gathering of two or more light workers in public places. At first light workers complied, but they were social beings and doing so went against their true selves. By that time, their existence had become so miserable that they created masks: a false one to wear when in public among dark workers and a true one they hoped would preserve their precious gifts. But it didn't work. It only weakened their ethereal forms. Finally, the only place they could find any relief was in their dreams and fantasies. So that's where they began to live. Those were the only things left they could control. The stress that resulted caused pent-up frustration, bitter resentment, dashed hopes and crushed ambitions.

"Except for a few older deities like DaValla and Julian, most forgot how to be in touch with their own and others feelings and emotions. They forgot how to make the connection to make thoughts real, let alone keep them in check or use them to help make wise decisions. Karoon was overjoyed. I suppose he thought his troubles were finally behind him.

"At about the same time, the City became so populated that it was difficult to know how many light workers were there. Concerned for his own welfare, Karoon decreed that certain improvements be made. That's when Sun City was split into four sections, tiers, with boundaries that unfairly deprived light workers of comforts bestowed upon dark workers."

Ra had been listening intently. "Yes, I remember how the scenery changed as I walked along that long street."

"That's right," Tobias replied stiffly. "That long street runs throughout the four tiers of the City. Aaru is located in what's known as the Zone. Before Karoon arrived, the sky over the entire City was a vibrant pink and turquoise blue and all sections of the street were paved in gold and in perfect condition. Immediately following the surrender, things changed in the worst way.

"Once a place where the air was exquisitely cool and so clean that it sparkled, Aaru is now just an open space on the lowest tier on the East side where the surface of the street is rocky and filled with pot holes. Not much better in quality, the next section is called the Pitts. Light workers live there in wretched dwellings. The sky over that section is still a vibrant pink and turquoise blue, reflections of their true cheerful natures, but the street is unpaved and rutted. The part of the street that runs through the next section, Mid-City, is paved and clean. However, a mist with a fetid odor and clammy feel plagues the area, and a perpetually gray sky dotted with puffy pouches of forest green looms over the dark workers who live there. You'll know you're in Karoonsville when the pavement turns to gold and is in perfect condition. But the sky here is dismal and dreary, with storm clouds that threaten and are always gray with patchy white layers.

"Morale was low and with time, more and more light workers tired of his unfair treatment. Besides worship and service, Karoon had no use for them, They were just trophies in his collection of conquests. That slight triggered something within the memory of a few of the older deities. They began to band together in small groups, protested the injustice that had been done. As it was in the time before his arrival, a few started thinking for themselves and caring for the welfare of each other but always in secret."

"That was just about when you arrived here in Sun City, wasn't it Tobias?" Julian observed.

Tobias nodded in agreement. "Yes, that's right. That's when I met the two of you." His violet eyes danced with the memory of that occasion. He looked at Ra and continued. "I wasn't affected quite as much as some. Julian, DaValla, myself, and a few others…we seem to have some kind of immunity. We're extremely careful about how we show our feelings and…"

"No emotional displays in the presence of any dark worker," observed DaValla. "Karoon couldn't prove it but he suspected there were some rebels who might find a way to influence the others, perhaps rekindle the protest about what was done to us. He was always on the lookout for a way to address problems before they happened."

"Catchers, Tobias. Tell him about catchers." Julian's high baritone voice sounded louder than normal.

"Where there were two or more light worker deities, there was also a catcher, a dark worker informer loyal to Karoon." A touch of sarcasm colored a quick chuckle. "Now there are so many catchers in Sun City that even Karoon can't remember them all.

"Sensitive to how colors and hues present, they secretly monitored the population, always on the lookout for abrupt or subtle changes that might signal discontent. Once exposed, Karoon found a way to handle the offender."

DaValla released a long sigh. "Handle as in banish to NoWhere. Karoon has always kept a tight rein on us. We want to be given the freedom he shows dark workers. But we are not all of one mind. Some want to proceed with caution. They excuse his indifference, believe he might have a change of heart. Others are more insistent and call for revolution. Unfortunately, we lack the means to go through with any such attempt."

Ra listened to DaValla's words, then asked Tobias, "Has anyone tried to get close enough to Karoon so that his energy field is infiltrated? That might do the trick."

"We've tried to get close enough to heap praise and worship upon him, let our positive energy wash over him, perhaps transform his darker vibes into something honorable. There's only one time in the City when everyone comes together. That's when Karoon is in residence for an entire week here at The Court."

Julian grinned and said, "He loves pomp and pageantry. Stately gatherings and non-stop festivities mostly attended by dark workers. They can be absent-minded, unstable, annoying and provocative. Even so, Karoon seems to bask in the satisfaction that comes with what their colors signify—unquestioning loyalty and worship of him. He grins and claps when they bow their misshapen forms before him and give him credit for performing fantastic deeds only imagined in their minds. Illusion. All illusion. They seem spellbound by his very presence. We've watched the spectacle from the sidelines, tried to break through the crowds of dark workers who surrounded him. But they used their vibes to keep us at a distance. Muddy yellow and forest green with dull gray splashes…ugh…repulsive!"

DaValla had been sitting quietly listening as Tobias and Julian spoke. "Actions born of desperation are often doomed to fail. He's not worthy of our respect and in response, many light workers are looking for a savior and would even consider trusting dark workers who smile at them, whisper supportive words in secret, make false promises to break the chains that hold us in bondage. There's a climate of unrest. Our City is divided. Deities are choosing sides, preparing for the clash which is sure to happen. I suspect that Karoon knows time is running out for him to devise a better way to exert control."

Tobias nodded in agreement, then added, "Yes, I wonder if that's why he failed to notice what was happening on that small planet he falsely took credit for creating—Earth."

Chapter 20

DaValla turned his gaze toward Ra. His silver-gray eyes grew small as he bristled, "Convinced of his absolute power and greatness, Karoon's inflated sense of accomplishment went into high gear. No longer satisfied to stop with the title of conqueror, he claimed he created planets. Just spoke them into existence. He demanded that everyone call him the Almighty, Greatest Creator God of all time! He claimed planet Earth was a testament to his power and glory, called the creatures who lived there, humans and considered them his children. To guarantee absolute control, only dark workers were allowed to interact with them. They were his police force and advanced his vibes but …"

When DaValla's voice trailed off into silence, Tobias spoke up. "There weren't enough dark workers to get the job done. Humans, like light workers, were an independent lot. After years of struggle and conflict, of making mistakes and learning from those mistakes, they understood the importance of discipline and control and how a lack of it could create problems. They also understood the importance of checks and balances, of not handing-over their free will to any individual or group who might have a self-serving purpose. They didn't take kindly to anyone or anything seeking to regulate their vibe. Not without a fight. Of course, there were exceptions. Some humans weren't concerned, especially those who didn't have their lives together. Some lacked a moral compass, went with what was right or wrong like a leaf in the wind.

"Some humans organized in a resistance movement they called the underground. They took whatever steps they could to protect themselves, all done in secret with the assistance of a few of us here in Sun City. Karoon's human minions tried to track them down but their efforts were not always consistent or effective. The result was that things didn't go as he planned."

DaValla gave the conference table a swipe with his fingers. "He wanted a way to punish humans, make them suffer for their disobedience. Then a few dark workers requested an audience with him to present a possible solution, at least as far as Earth was concerned.

"Normalizing.

"Power. Glory. Conquest. Desires that fueled selfish and irresponsible behavior—all features of the dark workers who approached Karoon.

"They compiled a list of humans already under their influence: power brokers with influence and connections, top military and political figures strategically placed world wide in key positions of every country on every continent. Then they conducted a test where a thermonuclear bomb was detonated about thirty-five miles on Earth above some isolated spot in one of their oceans, the Atlantic Ocean. It reached out into space, created gaps in the magnetic field that protected the surface from events like solar storms and so on. The explosion produced pulses of energy, electromagnetic radiation. It created a powerful electronic field around the planet, called an EMF, which even short-circuited their electronic equipment for brief periods of time.

"That test was an unexpected windfall for the dark workers. They'd been looking for a way to thin out the population and get rid of those who weren't loyal to Karoon, especially members of the underground who worked in secret with us to make the Earth a decent place to live.

"What happened encouraged the dark workers to go one step further. The humans under their control built a satellite with panels that collected energy from the sun, then converted it into electrical energy and found a way to move it back to Earth through the gaps that had already been created in the magnetic field. They developed a whole technology around it. Electrical energy converted into electromagnetic energy, EMP's, sent out in the form of shockwaves with one purpose: to break down the protective coating around cells in the human brain where emotions and feelings connect. It caused a kind of emotional detachment, that caused humans to forget how good it felt to be nice to each other. They lost their moral compass. The kind of destructive anti-social behavior Karoon approved of became commonplace regardless of the stress, confusion or despair that followed—for themselves or others. Conversion, the ultimate method of control. Normalizing, that's what Karoon called it."

After a second of silence, Tobias looked at Ra and said, "Time and space are relative. The distance between Sun City and Earth is closer than most imagine. We believe the control station is located right here in this very building. That's where dark workers monitor the satellite, schedule events, receive updates about the status of things on Earth and..." The expression on his face transformed into a stiff, tight-lipped scowl, "sometimes carry out experiments on us. They've tried various methods on a few light workers but something's missing or they're doing something wrong. When they figure it out—perfect it—we're doomed!" A sense of urgency clouded Tobias' voice. "We don't know where the energy is stored, but we need to find out because that's where the conversion happens."

"Is the effect permanent?"

"No, it gradually wears off humans who are already normalized. That's why they have event schedules. They release those pulses at regular intervals, about every twelve of their hours, to keep the effect going."

A crooked half-smile made its way across one corner of Tobias' lips then quickly disappeared. "Karoon would never suspect there are a few dark workers who have no love for him and are sympathetic to our cause. They go where we can't and feed us information. They've found glitches in those schedules, short intervals between scheduled start times and when they actually happen. They get the word out to us, and we pass it on to leaders in the underground on Earth. That's how some remain untouched. They alert others in their areas. They're all skilled in what they call the use of shielding technology. That warning gives them time to distance themselves from any electronic device that might become compromised and speed up the infection process. They move to safe rooms, shut off breakers, turn off Wi-Fi's, get away from anything that's metal. Some have invested in personal protective devices like EMP blankets, bracelets, pendants, all designed to render the shockwaves harmless. I guess you could say its an early warning system.

"There's one other thing. It has to do with untouched humans. The symbol of Karoon's authority is an ostrich feather. He claims it represents truth—his truth, his vibe. All currency on Earth bears a likeness of that image. All humans under his influence are permanently tattooed on their right forearms with that image. The untouched have developed a way to move about unnoticed. It's actually quite creative. They reproduce his sanctioned image on a piece of paper coated with some kind of film, then transfer it to their skin. But it's only a temporary tattoo and they have to remember to reapply the process if it washes off for some reason. They use the same method to identify each other when they get together in safe spaces, only they invert the hollow shaft of the feather, flip it so it points upwards. It's tricky. Spies are everywhere. And one slip gives them away."

Chapter 21

Tobias felt his lips tighten and form into a little twisted smile. He paused, then continued. "Networking. Dark workers do that well. We've learned a lot by watching them. If they only knew how we use it to our advantage.

"Right now, dark workers are connecting with humans under their control in an attempt to target the remaining rebels in a place called Jamaica. If Karoon can convert them, we'll be his next target. If he suspects that a few of us are not what we pretend to be, that the memory of being in tune with feelings and emotions hasn't entirely abandoned our population, then rather than root out individuals, he will penalize everyone. He might try and use those EMP shockwaves on us, but our forms are energetic, our particles much finer than the energy fields of humans. Our vibes resonate to a different, higher frequency, and those waves would pass right through us. We must stay in control, keep the boundaries of our energy fields well-defined, and protect those of us in positions to someday make a difference."

A long, deep sigh escaped from between Tobias's lips. When he spoke, his voice took on a mystical quality as if he was lost in a critique of his own tactical prowess.

"Karoon is unsure about who I am, my true self. He's heard that I'm a light worker, a Singularity, but also thinks I'm desperate for the few perks and privileges he dispenses. I've fooled him into believing that I'm his personal agent, that I support his means and methods. That couldn't be further from the truth. The way he acts, the things he does, I have reason to suspect that's not who he truly is. Everyone makes mistakes. For the present, I'll reserve my judgement."

Tobias turned and studied Ra carefully. When he spoke again, his words took the form of a guarded invitation. "We've presented our case. Can we count on you to help with our cause?"

Having posed his question, Tobias watched Ra for a long second without speaking and thought, *This is the second time patches of greenish gray flecks color your bright violet and lavender hues. Think carefully, sprite. This is a defining moment in your journey...one way or the other.*

The silence in the room was deafening.

Not to be put off by Ra's lack of response, Tobias continued. "There's much more to tell you. And another request to make, but we have to be careful. There are information leaks, those among us who have no honor, spies, catchers and …"

The metallic clack of chairs that bumped against the conference table in Karoon's office suite abruptly halted the conversation.

Tobias strained to hear more. "Just a minute," he whispered, then rose from his chair, walked toward the door, and shouted, "Who's out there?"

Chapter 22

A male was hiding in the shadows of Karoon's office suite. It was Anwir, a light worker turned darker worker catcher. He patiently trolled the shadows. Bided his time.

Anwir wasn't exactly sure how old Tobias was. From his appearance, he figured they were closer in age than the others on the Council. But that was as far as it went.

There was a time when he and Tobias were comrades, shared one truth and a common vision. But with Karoon's arrival and impatient for change, the low road he eventually chose was not destined for enlightenment.

Anwir took great pains to camouflage the layers of what had become his greenish gray energy field with masses of bright yellow. When it worked, the overall effect was magical.

The only problem was that he did not know how much longer he could keep up the pretense and make Tobias believe he still shared his passion enough to let his guard down and speak freely in his presence.

As luck would have it, he bumped into Isfet in the lobby as he walked away from the elevator after his unplanned run-in with Ra and Tobias in the hallway.

Practically bubbling over with childish glee, Isfet raced toward Anwir, jacket of his tacky dark-blue pinstripe suit billowing around him, anxious to make the kind of announcement he was famous for.

"Ra is in the building! Ra is in the building!"

"Really?" Anwir's jet-black eyes grew wide as he digested Isfet's words. He casually twisted and untwisted the gold chain around his neck as he observed Isfet, wondering what kind of mischief he planned.

"Did you know Ra is from the second plane?"

"Who told you that?"

"Karoon himself."

Always through you, he mused. *Never directly to me. I'm just poor Anwir...an afterthought, not good enough to run in your circle.*

Anwir was well aware of how things worked at The Court between himself, Karoon and Isfet. He thought membership on the Inner Council gave him some kind of status, at least made him a useful source of information. But the reality was he would never share their confidence. As far as Karoon was concerned, trust was important...but loyalty meant everything. And it must be proven. Isfet had never violated that loyalty. But it was common knowledge that Anwir and Tobias had once been close and that he betrayed that friendship. As low as they had all fallen, there was nothing worse than a traitor.

Anwir was silent as he considered Isfet's announcement. *This deity, Ra. So new to the scene, on probation and already favored by Karoon over those he has history with. What is Karoon up to? Ra was sent to Sun City to do a job, but what job? Important? Definitely, for Karoon to send a deity from the second plane.* He vowed to get to Ra before Tobias and the others did to discover where his sentiments lay.

"Well, where is he?" he growled.

With his lips closed, Isfet raised one corner of his mouth to form a small half smile, then calmly answered, "He's with

Tobias. Up on the tenth floor. Oh, and by the way, guess who I just saw getting into the elevator?"

The suspense was actually killing him but Anwir remained aloof. "I couldn't imagine"

"DaValla and Julian headed up that way, too."

Anwir's muffled gasps caused every sound in the lobby to go quiet. "Members of the Inner Council," he railed, "all together on the tenth floor and with Ra!" *They're having a meeting? Why wasn't I invited?* The thought made its way across Anwir's lips to Isfet's ears before he could stop it.

Isfet's blood red eyes twinkled. He feigned innocence and croaked, low and rough, "I don't know," as he thought, *Now, there's a little mystery for you to figure out.*

Chapter 23

Anwir made his way to the tenth floor. He paced the hallway for a few seconds, then entered Karoon's office suite. The corners of his mouth curved into a humorless smile as his mind constructed a fantasy of epic proportions. *Tobias wouldn't dare risk having it get back to Karoon that his space was used for unofficial business without his permission. If they are holding a meeting, it's probably back in that little room behind the conference table. That Tobias… I don't trust him. Wouldn't it be wonderful if I could hide near the door in the shadows, eavesdrop, maybe overhear a word, phrase, anything that might prove…marketable. Then, at the right moment, make a grand entrance and savor their reaction.*

Unfortunately, his collision with the chairs and the conference table in Karoon's office suite brought that possibility to an abrupt halt.

Anwir froze, then whirled around in a startled panic. He tried to shrink his energy field in so close that he couldn't be noticed, but it was no use. Exposed as he was, he put on his best false-faced smile and answered Tobias, his voice gravely calm. "It's me, Anwir. I was just passing by and noticed, uh, the door was open, so I thought there might be an intruder in here. You know how particular Karoon is about security. But, you're having a meeting? Evidently my invitation…"

"…must have gotten lost in the mail." The muscles around Tobias' mouth forced a smile as he finished Anwir's sentence. "Please join us. We were just getting acquainted."

For a second, Anwir looked confused. Thin wispy streaks of red and black snaked through the bright yellow layers of the energy field he constructed, changed his appearance from magical to something that was murky and strangely disturbing. He realized what happened and tried to make the necessary corrections before anyone noticed, even expanded his energy field to make himself look more intimidating than he actually was. But it was too late. Aware that all eyes were trained on him, he eased into the room and sat in one of the unoccupied chairs. Finally he turned toward Ra and said in a voice that was more raspy than usual, "Well, well, you must be the deity of the hour."

That voice—deep, arrogant, and strangely familiar. Ra raised his chin and replied, "I wouldn't go so far as all that. Say, your voice sounds familiar. Have we met before?"

Anwir avoided Ra's gaze. Instead, his eyes darted nervously back and forth. "No, don't believe I've had the pleasure," he said, and reluctantly extended his hand across the for a handshake.

Ra returned the gesture, but showed little enthusiasm. Instead he found himself shooting Tobias a quick glance, one that wasn't returned.

Somehow, they made it through the introductions. With each deity in a seat at the table, the conversation continued, but on a much different note.

Anwir wasted no time with pleasantries.

"So, Ra, what's your position on the way things are here in Sun City?"

Ra took his time before answering. First, he cleared his throat with a closed-mouth cough. Then he crossed one leg over the other, cocked his head to one side and glanced upward towards the ceiling. He eyed Anwir suspiciously and replied, "I really haven't given it much thought." With a dismissive wave of his hand, he continued. "If you don't mind, I'd rather focus on this planet Earth matter. I understand the situation down there has deteriorated?"

"I believe that's correct," Anwir observed drily. "Karoon told me that the focus of his human creations has shifted from what he expected it to be."

The expression on Ra's face grew somber. He sighed and said, "That's why I'm going—"

"Down there to clean things up." All heads turned toward the speaker, Anwir, who unfortunately let impatience get the best of him.

Frantic to recover from a gross slip of the tongue, Anwir gave a nervous laugh and muttered, "Oh, yes, well, I mean…I just assumed that…what I meant to say was I don't understand why Karoon thinks it necessary for a deity to go down to that cesspool of a planet." He smirked and said, "I would never do that."

Always ready to perform before an audience, Anwir became more animated. He waved one long finger in the air and launched into a rant. "Like I said, I wouldn't set foot in that place. There was a time not so long ago when a huge flood almost wiped all those arrogant little bastards from the face of that planet. Pity that wasn't successful." His raspy voice dissolved into a deep chuckle. "Unfortunately, enough survived to repopulate."

The mellow sound of Tobias' rich baritone voice suddenly took on a flavor that sizzled like molten white-hot lava.

"Arrogant little bastards?" he growled. "I remind you of Karoon's mandate, that only dark workers are allowed to interact with humans. Are you implying he would give dark workers any task that was beneath them?"

DaValla turned his gaze toward the window. His silver-gray eyes became steely as he peered out, pretended to search the skyline for some unidentified point of reference.

Julian just sat there. First to DaValla then back to Tobias, his hazel eyes darted back and forth like those of a caged animal desperate to escape captivity.

Anwir squirmed in his chair, seemingly indifferent to how his breaths had suddenly deteriorated into short, shallow wheezing.

This time it was Ra who broke the silence. With his head cocked to one side, he studied both Tobias and Anwir, then calmly observed, "Anwir, it sounds like you don't care much for humans. Do you?"

"Well, of course I do." *If that's what you want to hear me say.* The icy stare of his eyes, black as obsidian, bored into Ra. "It's just that instead of going himself and getting his hands dirty, he prefers to send you, a candidate on probation."

Ra's brows drew together. He scoffed and murmured, "That was his decision."

"And what will you do when you get there?"

"Whatever it takes to get the job done."

Chapter 24

The last thing Tobias wanted was to confirm any suspicion Anwir might have about clandestine meetings. But it was getting more difficult to sit back in silence and endure his dishonorable behavior. Aside from his breathing becoming slow and steady, Tobias gave no reaction to the tension that filled the air. His eyes searched the layers of Anwir's energy field for clues that might reveal the presence of the kind of joy that comes with discovering secret information, then hid themselves behind a mask of detachment. *I must remember the reason why we are gathered here,* he thought. *It's more about Ra than Anwir. I need to know how a tense situation like this affects him.*

Tobias wasn't the only one concerned about the turn of the conversation's tone. Ra had remained silent for a long second, watching every move Tobias made. *I wondered how he would handle this awkward situation. Well played, Tobias, well played. I'd love to know the real you behind the mask you wear. You've certainly got what it takes to be a great leader. I could learn a lot from you.* So it wasn't hard to imagine his surprise when he heard the echo of a familiar smooth, deep velvety baritone voice tumble into his mind in the form of a thought.

Thanks. I've always believed that when the student is ready, the teacher will appear.

Ra's face paled as he thought, *It's happening again, just like with Lynette.* When his eyes locked on Tobias' face like magnets, a look passed between them that spoke volumes. Tobias smiled, and Ra knew a connection had been established with another deity. *We're little more than strangers,* Ra thought, *but something about Tobias' energy field has brought us together with the ability to understand through each other's experience. I'll test the strength of the connection. Tobias, I'll bet you're wondering how much of our conversation Anwir overheard?*

That's exactly what I'm wondering.

So, we're actually having a thought conversation?

Yes, we are.

Alright. I've got a few questions for you. Correct me if I'm wrong, but that door wasn't open. It was closed!

That's right.

What Anwir said about my going down to Earth to clean things up. Those are the same words I used with Isfet in the lobby. How could Anwir repeat them, and so accurately?

We've known for a long time that Isfet and Anwir collaborate. That's why we're so careful about what we say when he's around. He usually avoids doing anything that would expose their connection. I'm surprised he let his guard down in front of you.

The words were straightforward enough, but somewhere in his tone, Ra sensed a bittersweet note.

Tobias, I felt the vibration that ran through your essence when Anwir talked about humans. It made me almost want to vomit.

Yes, that's what happens when I'm close to my boiling point. You're really the curious type.

This is the last question for now. Tobias, why didn't you return the glance I shot you when Anwir reached out to shake my hand? You must have felt my disgust at the touch of his long, cold fingers. They made me cringe.

Tobias paused, then thought, *I felt your desire to pull away from him. I'm not here to offer you sympathy, but to challenge you to consider the wisdom of decisions you make, because there will always be consequences.*

Chapter 25

Sensing the conversation was about to spiral into chaos, DaValla decided it was time for an intervention. He turned toward Ra and asked, "Have you picked a destination?"

"I'm open for suggestions."

"Jamaica. I'd suggest going to Kingston, Jamaica."

"Kingston? Is that one of their cities?"

"Yes, it is. It's the capital and the largest city. It's on the southeastern coast of the island."

Eager to establish a position of authority in the conversation, Anwir said, "Capital cities are always popular destination choices—repositories of culture as well as power. But, I'm curious." Turning to face DaValla, he asked, "Why do you suggest Kingston? What's so special about Kingston?"

DaValla felt a chill run up his spine. *Did Anwir hear Tobias mention Jamaica during our secret conversation?* Ra, unaccompanied, would be open to attack by any dark worker looking to build a reputation, including Isfet. What if he got into trouble and couldn't complete the mission? Duty, obligation, and a growing fondness for Ra caused him to now consider himself, along with Tobias and Julian, as Ra's advance guard. It would be their honor to pave the way for him, help him use available resources to his advantage, remind him to stay in control. But his decision to proceed without them undermined their roles as his protectors. That left them with only one option: prepare him while he was still with them.

DaValla knew all too well the danger of appearing more informed than a dark worker. He watched Anwir thoughtfully, then said, "Oh, I don't know. It's just that, being the capital, well, I imagine that in the beginning, the creator picked a few locations and endowed them with special qualities. It's my understanding that Atlantis was such a place due to its wealth and advanced civilization. So, it's quite possible that the island continent of Jamaica was also one of those places. Mountains, hills, coastal plains, and interior valleys. A wealth of precious stones, metals, and exotic creatures. Plant life of such beauty that it rivaled any found in our heavenly gardens. In the beginning, the creator gave them everything needed to maintain balance and support life."

Annoyed by the comment, Anwir's forehead knotted in an angry frown. "Just a minute. Are you implying Karoon didn't create that planet?"

Sensing an opportunity to unsettle Anwir enough to turn the conversation to his advantage, DaValla faked a smile and replied, "Not at all. I only said, in the beginning."

That's it, shut him down! Julian remained silent, but the humor in the look he shot DaValla was hard to misinterpret.

Anwir's arrogant attitude quickly faded. "Well…all right, proceed."

"As I was saying, at some point humans started building luxurious all-inclusive resorts, spectacular beach attractions, preparing outstanding cuisine, things they evidently enjoyed doing. Things they deemed made life worth living. I could be wrong, but I don't think that was entirely what Karoon had in mind." He looked at Anwir and asked, "Do you agree?"

"I hardly think so. What's your point?"

"It was around that time when the normalizing process began. How Karoon must have felt. Why, the very idea of them abandoning him, their—" The contemptuous glint in his silver-gray eyes made its way into his voice as he spat the word that finished the sentence, "creator. I heard Karoon wasn't too happy about that slight. Perhaps a severe consequence, some sort of punishment, was in order? I don't believe they knew anything about gang warfare, drug and sex trafficking, poverty or social unrest until normalizing was imposed."

Julian gazed at DaValla and thought, *Didn't know how skilled you were at using diplomacy to let the truth be known.*

Gathering his composure, DaValla continued. "A few humans, the untouched, objected to his consequences. Karoon called them rebels. They wanted to go their own way free of his control. That's what he's concerned about."

Satisfied with the explanation, DaValla fixed his gaze on Ra and said, "If you're going down there, you'll need a male human body suit to contain your essence." Aware of Anwar's presence and suddenly feeling very vulnerable, he continued. "If I might make a suggestion. I don't like to spread gossip, but there's talk that some deities in Sun City have unregulated access to information about humans—what they call profiles—hobbies, work, favorite social activities, and so on. If those profiles could be located, that might be a place to start looking for a suitable candidate. It might also help us learn how to communicate better with them."

Anwir's black obsidian eyes grew wide as he growled, "Where did you hear that?"

"Oh, I don't remember. Possibly a conversation between dark workers overheard in passing. You know how it is when you're so involved with your work that it occupies every thought."

Seemingly unaware of the slight, Anwir replied, "Yes, well, I can appreciate that."

Ra's brows knitted together. "How would I communicate with a human?"

Although he already knew the answer, DaValla's reply was quite guarded. "Oh, it's forbidden for a light worker to have contact with a human. I can't speak from experience but I do believe it's possible. It's all about energy.

Ra nodded. "That should prove interesting. I'll look forward to it."

Pleased by his quick thinking, a faint smile made its way across DaValla's lips into his silver-gray eyes. "Perhaps there's a human in Jamaica…a male…yes, a local. If I had a choice, which of course I don't, but if, I would choose someone with certain qualities. After all, he's going to act as a kind of mentor, a resource to you while in his body. Perhaps a lawyer, intelligent, good-natured, very humble about his achievements. An ordinary man. A man of the people!"

A slight movement in the muscles of his face was enough to pull DaValla's pouty lips upward into a tiny half-smile. Just as the tension at the corners of his mouth approached the point of no return, he wished it away before Anwir could notice the change in his expression. It was, after all, just a communication to himself, a reminder that the darkness had not yet swallowed all in them that was decent. Fully recovered, he crinkled his nose, furrowed his brow and said, "That would be a windfall."

A cold smile spread across Anwir's lips and found its way into his black, obsidian eyes. "It would be nice if he turned out to be a rebel. Why, he might even lead us to their headquarters!"

Amazed at his obvious misinterpretation, DaValla shook his head in the affirmative. "Yes, Anwir. It would be." Then he looked at Ra and said, "Are you with me so far?"

The bright violet and lavender blue layers of Ra's energy field were momentarily obscured by flashes of indigo. Each massive pulse expanded and contracted with the explosive force of a supernova.

"But what if things go wrong? My entry into the human will be a delicate operation. If he's not prepared, the consequences might be disastrous. Are you certain he will have no problem with me just moving in?"

Anwir smirked and said, "There's already been talk of one human who might fit the bill. George Patel. He's at a crossroads in his life. He might actually appreciate the experience."

How could there have already been talk about the human if we're only now having the conversation, wondered DaValla. Directing his attention toward Anwir, he restated Ra's concern, "But, what if the human resists?"

Anwir considered that possibility with mixed emotions. "Well, uh, just assert your authority and…" Suddenly at a loss for words, his deep, raspy voice trailed off. He sat there and silently fingered the links in his gold bracelet.

"I'll deal with that, if it happens." Ra's reply was swift and unemotional. "Anwir, you'll provide this profile information for my review before I depart?"

"Of course, Ra."

"Along with other information about humans," added DaValla. "Facts about their living spaces, how they interact, common words and phrases, and so on. I'm sure you'll return with much information to increase our bank of knowledge. By the way, the official language is English, but you'll need to understand those who speak Jamaican patois, a version of English that developed there."

Only DaValla was wise enough to appreciate how making a mistake could not only jeopardize the success of the mission, but take away privileges. At least for himself, Julian, and Tobias.

"One moment, Ra. There is one final thing we need to consider. It might be best to designate one of us as a contact on this end to relay messages. Just to cut down on the confusion."

Well-meaning as he was, freedom-loving Julian lacked not only the desire but the discipline for such a responsibility.

DaValla posed the question but didn't volunteer for the job. He knew the danger accepting that duty would put him in, especially with Anwir listening. Lessons learned during his many years had taught him the wisdom of maintaining a low profile unless absolutely necessary to do otherwise.

That left Tobias.

Turning to face Tobias, DaValla exclaimed, "You are probably the logical choice."

Eager to have the spotlight move away from himself, Julian seconded the nomination. "Yes, Tobias should be the one. That makes sense. Then we all agree?"

Yes. Yes. Flashes. Swirls. Whirls and spirals. The space they occupied was once again aglow with luminous bright yellow. With one exception—Anwir.

Anwir assumed his best false-faced smile. His voice came out in a raspy complaint. "Wait a minute. How about me? Don't you think I'm capable of handling that job?"

"No doubt whatsoever," responded DaValla, "but I think you could use your talents for something more important. Why don't you inform the human body suit that Ra is coming and make sure he knows what to expect."

Anwir flashed a toothy grin. "A fine suggestion. No doubt the human body suit will consider my contact an honor. Tobias might do the job. As efficient as he is. But there's no need to let my expertise go to waste."

Trying his best to look stoic, DaValla thought, *Dangerous, diabolical expertise is more like it.*

Without so much as a pause, DaValla interjected, "Yes, Anwir, your efforts will certainly pave the way for success."

Suspicious of his eagerness to be helpful, DaValla made a mental note to remember Anwir's agreement. *I'll personally make a memorandum for the record. The consequence of him not keeping his bargain could be devastating for both Ra and the human body suit.*

Chapter 26

Satisfied with how things were progressing, Ra's energy field once again rippled with layers of bright violet and lavender blue. Sensing the meeting was about to come to an end, he made a final observation about informing the human body suit prior to his arrival.

"That should make my task much easier. I'd like the human to react like we are old friends picking up where we left off following a long separation. With a bond of friendship and trust already in place, he won't fear my essence being in his body. He will follow my lead without question or complaint."

Once the scheme had been laid, the meeting concluded. Everyone went their separate ways, with the exception of Ra and Tobias.

Thinking Anwir might decide to return, Ra moved closer to Tobias. In a rushed pace that was uncharacteristic of him, he whispered, "I had a feeling there was something else you wanted to say but didn't. What stopped you?"

"I couldn't be totally open with Anwir sitting in the room. But George Patel is the leader of the untouched in Jamaica. He's who we had in mind all along," *and the conduit for the secret you need to learn to fulfill your destiny.* "I didn't want to confirm Anwir's suspicion that some of us have relationships with humans. I don't agree with that comment he made about you exerting your authority. This will be a joint effort. There's something you should know. Human bodies are thicker than ours because their environment is different. By the way, George is still in touch with his feelings and emotions."

"Feelings and emotions made real?"

"Yes. Even though he's from a lower plane, you'll hold conversations, send messages back and forth. George will hear your voice in his mind. You'll pick up on thoughts and sensations within his body and experience them as though they were your own. He'll help you label them so you can bridge the gap between thoughts, feelings, and emotions. You could even use his vocal cords to form your thoughts into spoken words, although probably in a voice that sounds different from your own. This will assault your essence because you've never experienced anything in that way. You'll be out of your comfort zone and have to make certain adjustments. Otherwise, you'll constantly be disoriented and distracted. Don't panic. Stay in control. If it happens, discuss it with George. Ask him how peace-of-mind prevents emotional overload. He's a teacher's teacher, honorable and an excellent role model. Treat him with respect. Remember, you'll be a guest in his body."

Ra nodded his head in agreement.

"Now, about that request. Our agenda is obviously different than the one Anwir and Karoon would have you accomplish. We want you to open yourself to George's experience. Try to see things from his perspective. Don't use what you find to trap and punish. Learn the secret. Be a vessel for that knowledge. Bring it back to the Heavenly Realm. You'll know what to do with it…when the time is right."

His curiosity piqued, Ra asked, "And normalizing? How exactly does George Patel avoid being normalized?"

"Humans can't avoid that on their own. George is a leader. He receives an advance alarm so he can get the word out to others before an event happens. He takes precautions. He always wears a black EMP bracelet on his left arm. Concealed, of course."

Ra was too proud to meet Tobias's heartfelt gaze with eyes that showed outright reluctance. Things were becoming complicated. He'd sworn an oath of loyalty to Karoon and now he was having second thoughts. *I hate to disappoint Tobias, but I'm not sure I want to get involved in all this drama. Maybe I should go back home and figure another way to make a name for myself.*

Lost in thought, Ra glanced at the floor, searched for an excuse to back out gracefully. "On second thought, I don't know if I'm ready for all of this. There's so much that I have to learn; and, what if—"

"Ra, please hear me out. I am acquainted with the laws and mores that govern second plane deities. They frown on contact outside your colonies. Your elders demand that you keep the edges of your own energy fields well-defined. They have mastered the art of discipline and control, and expect sprites to do the same. You'll be the first to challenge this tradition. The prospect might seem unnerving, but you'll not be harmed. Have faith. Your energy field won't be infiltrated if you stay focused and…," Tobias paused. The next words he spoke held a tone used only by those with perfect and unfaltering belief in the truth of their statements. He gazed deeply into Ra's emerald green orbs for a long second, then inhaled, slowly released the breath and said, "You're capable of handling the adjustment process. The real issue is that you don't know who you are or what you want."

"I…"

"Your own journey has just begun, and here I am asking you to fight for the well-being of others. Even at risk to yourself."

Tobias shook his head in disbelief. "Your elders keep sprites close to them far too long. They keep you dependent upon them. In a way, they're like Karoon, only not as heartless about it. You're a rebel, full of contradictions, with too many voices screaming at you. Who should you listen to? Should you please your elders or risk their ridicule? A taste for adventure, excitement, new experiences. Those desires are like a beast within you. Until you tame them, learn from them, use them to help you step into your power and own it—they remain your enemy. You're like a child with a new toy who lacks the insight to know what to do with it."

"There's something else. I've sworn an oath of loyalty to Karoon. You're asking me to break it."

It's time, thought Tobias. *The student is ready.*

What's happening to me? For a second Ra felt himself swept up in the intensity of Tobias' violet-orbed stare. It grabbed and held him, caused him to feel like they had become one, drained him of all guilt and self-doubt, then infused him with courage and confidence. Precursors of power.

Tobias' eyes opened wide as he noted Ra's reaction, then continued. "Rebels are often born leaders, powerful in their own right. I suspect that one day you will understand this. Everyone makes mistakes. Right now, your character is like the blade of a sword that's being forged. You lack the experience needed for tempering. But, that's alright. All I ask is that you believe in yourself as I believe in you. Your presence here is not by accident. You've come a long way. Now you must chose the road you will travel.

With words of encouragement couched in the sound of a smooth, deep, velvety baritone voice, Tobias continued. "If—when you decide to move forward, consider this: Karoon's agenda is clear. He has given you a directive that will advance it. But you're just starting your career, building your reputation. What he wants from you…is that how you want to be remembered? I'm offering you a chance to be celebrated as the one who worked to create something greater than himself. It's your choice; but something about you makes me know you'll take the high road. The formality of a ritual is unnecessary." Tobias paused for a second, then added, "Besides, you have me, *us,* in your corner."

"Can you guarantee that I won't be harmed?"

The infectious smile that spread across Tobias' lips found its way into his violet eyes. "Well, let's just say that what I predict about the future always comes true. The prospect might seem unnerving; but, if your energy field is infiltrated, you won't be harmed. Trust me—I mean, us. We light worker deities have to stick together. If things really get bad, I…we can safely pull you back. Stay focused, and don't give in to temptation."

Tobias's words, his candid plea touched something deep within Ra's essence. *He's genuinely concerned for my welfare.* Ra grinned and replied," So, now I'm a light worker?"

"Yes, you are." When Tobias felt Ra's vibes lift, his own demeanor relaxed. "Who knows," he chuckled. "I wouldn't be surprised to find that service to others over self is your true calling. Possibly even your destiny."

Ra didn't want to believe he had been deceived, that Karoon wasn't worthy of his respect. Then he remembered the unsettled feel of Karoon's embrace and reference to finding information that needed to be kept confidential.

But the legacy Tobias spoke of …

The bright violet and lavender blue hues of his energy field glowed. Ra turned to face Tobias and declared, "Your vibe…now mine! Alright, I'm in."

Tobias reached out and embraced Ra with all the respect and deference shown by one warrior to another. Enfolded within the layers of his energy field—gold, tinged with white and purple—Ra absorbed the favor bestowed upon him, unaware of the supreme blessing conferred.

Anwir never intended to keep the promise he made to the Council. He didn't care one way or the other if the human body suit was prepared to accept Ra. In fact, he preferred that it be a surprise to the human, just to see how the deity of the hour would handle the pressure.

He couldn't wait to leave the meeting with Tobias and the others. There was a contact to make.

The catcher in Anwir was fully activated. *Tobias and Ra. When I left, they were still in that room. Tobias claims he supports Karoon's plan. But I know he doesn't. I just need a little more proof that he's been communicating with those human rebels down there. Then, I'll go to Karoon, reveal the truth about him. Karoon will make an example of him. Oh, how he will make Tobias suffer! And Ra! I don't trust him either. He didn't support my arrogant little bastard comment. Is he really going down there to clean things up the way Karoon wants it to happen? Well, I've got a surprise for them. Second plane deities. I know their strengths and weaknesses. I believe Ra's energy field can be compromised while he's in that human body suit. A male deity in a male human body suit. The perfect combination. Yes, desire will get the job done, starting with a very special human temptress…Vera.*

Part 2 - Vera

Chapter 27

Monday morning. Just past midnight. The night sky was clear enough to view the full arch of the Milky Way and busy enough to hide a bright violet and lavender flash of light as it raced toward planet Earth.

That flash of light was Ra.

Everything about Earth was foreign to him—the atmosphere, sights, sounds…humans. Until he could partner with the human body suit, his ethereal essence was just another wave of energy riding a beam of new moonlight. Like a deep-sea diver about to take a dip in the ocean, he was anxious to don protective gear, the human body suit guaranteed by Anwir.

The address of the complex given him by Tobias was easy to find. Mona Heights, a neighborhood in southeastern Saint Andrew Parish, about five miles from Kingston and not too far from the main campus of the University of the West Indies. The development wasn't new, but the units had been kept in good repair.

All was quiet, with the exception of a few men milling around the courtyard armed with M-16 assault rifles. The night air was sultry; still, they wore orange, bullet-proof vests, each with the word, SECURITY, spelled out in silver reflective tape bordered with contrasting trim.

Don't create a panic. Maintain a low profile. Easy enough to do, Ra thought as he toned his bright violet and lavender hues down until they were almost transparent, passed among them unnoticed, then made his way around swimming pools and through parking lots filled with sedan cars in various states of repair.

Upon seeing Building C, Ra knew he had arrived at his destination.

What he saw made his colors and hues sparkle with delight. *It's a good omen when windows and entrances face the East.* He made his way up the stairs two floors then stopped at Unit 211.

He passed through the exterior wall and once inside the unit, hesitated for a few seconds to get his bearings.

His advance guard back in Sun City had done what they could to prepare him for his journey. They briefed him on what they understood life must be like in Jamaica, enough to help him navigate on his own until he could find and partner with the human body suit. Small as his vocabulary was, he knew enough to recognize and label things found in human living spaces called homes. That's how he knew he stood in an entrance foyer. When he looked around, he could tell the area was divided into what humans called living spaces…rooms, grouped into sections according to their purpose, either for public activities or private use.

I'm near the entrance, a space most likely meant for public activities. Since no one else was around, he deliberated for a few seconds, then concluded the object of his search awaited him in a room somewhere in the private space.

Anxious to partner with the human male, Ra moved along the hallway that separated the rooms in the private space with the stealth of a tiger stalking its prey. Two rooms on one side, one on the other side.

He passed them all until he arrived at the last room on the left. That's where he stopped and hovered in the open doorway. *This private space must be used for sleeping—a bedroom,* he concluded. A smaller room was connected that housed a walk-in shower, medicine cabinet, pedestal washstand and toilet.

The only light came from a window across the room. Framed by floor to ceiling sheers, it overlooked the parking lot in front of the condo. The gentle breeze that blew from an air conditioner vent in the ceiling was just enough to move a few panels around, let faint fingers of moonlight filter through to reveal furnishings expected in a space used for resting.

A dresser, two matching nightstands, and plain table lamps. A wall closet with a full-length mirror hung on one side of the partially open door. Tailored suits and shirts, each one on its own hanger, with a necktie looped over it. Pairs of what humans called shoes, worn on their feet, appropriate for any occasion, neatly grouped in rows across the closet floor.

And, a special feature that didn't go unappreciated.

George Patal, the human male, and soon-to-be body suit.

Ra lingered for a moment and studied him with an almost childlike fascination.

The human lay face-up, stretched-out across a king-sized platform bed, partially covered by a crisp, white cotton sheet, head on a pillow and nude, presumably from the waist up. Finally, he made his way into the room. He edged closer and closer, hugged the walls until he hovered just a few inches above George's prone form.

Healthy, athletic, a perfect specimen. Dark brown skin, possibly tanned more from too much unprotected exposure to the sun. A black EMP bracelet on his left arm, and a small ostrich feather tattooed on his right forearm…flipped…hollow shaft pointed up.

Like a gentle river flowing into an ocean, Ra's essence slipped into George's body.

So far, so good. Not even a slight rise in his blood pressure. Pleased that the first hurdle had been accomplished with no problem, Ra opened a portal between them to test the strength of their connection.

Unfortunately, his appraisal was premature.

Almost immediately his essence was assaulted by a flood of sensations—images and sounds normal for humans but foreign to him. The sound of blood that coursed through a network of vessels. The thump of George's heart beat in his chest. The low-pitched, soft rustling sound of air that moved in and out of his lungs. Peculiar gurgling sounds as bits of food in varying degrees of digestion moved through his GI tract.

Alarmed, Ra quickly closed the portal. *Tobias was right. It's too much, too soon. I've got to find a way to tone it down.* He steeled himself, then opened it again. What happened next welcomed him to a new reality, far greater than anything he ever imagined.

Maybe he sensed Ra's complaint. Whatever the reason, George rolled over onto his stomach, then casually fluffed and repositioned his pillow so it covered his head. Doing so not only caused his body to relax, but also muted the attack on Ra.

"Ah, that's better," Ra whispered thankfully.

The scent that drifted from the pillow was what caught his attention. It reminded him of something shared from George's profile. Yes, George wore some kind of liquid on his neck and face, something human males called cologne. He even remembered the name—Atelier Pomelo Paradis. *I need to capture that particular scent, examine it, and understand how to appreciate it as George does. But what if it overwhelms me? If I have to make an adjustment, will it have the same meaning for me as it does for him?*

Ra isolated the part of George's brain that was his smell center and there it was—citrus, the scent of the cologne George wore. A rush of exotic odors passed through his essence: mandarin oranges from Italy; pomelo from France;

and Haitian vetiver. He suddenly felt happy because that's how the experience made George feel.

Then a peculiar thing happened. Without warning, another series of sensations hit him like a thunderbolt. Pressure. Warmth. Wetness. The back-and-forth motion of vibrations shooting up and down George's spine. All new to him, the intensity of it left Ra breathless and a little confused. *I'll have to remember to ask the human about that.* How could he know that the open portal allowed him entry into every aspect of George's internal experience, including his private fantasies. As shy as he was in real life, at that moment George was deep in the bliss of an erotic fantasy getting a blow job from a local woman he had never formally met but affectionately referred to as his dream lover.

The partnering process was well underway. The satisfaction Ra felt displayed in the bright violet and lavender hues of his energy field. He would have loved for the human to experience it, but that would not happen as long as he shared his body. Confidence in the success of his mission would have to be consolation enough. The second hurdle completed, this time with no problem.

Things were going well. It was hard for Ra to envision anything that would cause a turn for the worse. But it happened, brought about by something as simple as the sound of a car horn that honked outside in the parking lot, loud enough to jolt George out of his slumber and send mild low-frequency vibes throughout Ra's essence.

Ra didn't have to guess. He knew exactly what happened. Instead of the expected warm greeting, what he feared most had come true.

Anwir didn't keep his promise. George is not prepared. He's fighting back with all his strength and energy. Unless he calms down, the intensity of his struggle will result in injury to both of us, perhaps beyond repair for him. An unexpected twist, but nothing I can't handle—with a little course correction.

Chapter 28

George heard something that sounded like words but they were muffled and barely discernible.

"Human, don't be alarmed. I'm with you now."

A long sigh escaped his lips as he slid back down in his bed, pulled the sheet up over his shoulders, told himself that it was just mind chatter. *That's all it is, me talking to myself but it doesn't sound anything like my voice. It sounds tight-throated and thin, like someone struggling to find and connect words into coherent sentences…like me listening through an ear in my head to a voice moving swiftly through a tunnel!*

Pulling back one side of his pillow, George peeped out and cautiously surveyed the part of the room visible from where he lay. Seeing no one, he drew in a long breath, released it with an audible sigh into the emptiness surrounding him, then pushed the pillow aside.

He wiped the sleep from his eyes and murmured, "I must still be dreaming because I—"

Again, he heard the voice, this time deeper, the words clearer. "Please, remain calm."

Still not quite awake enough to know what was going on, George grew silent. As he pushed the sheet back, it was hard for his tan-colored pajama bottoms to conceal the well-endowed lower half of his body. His breath came in rapid, shallow whiffs. He tried to sit-up, but his usual agile form seemed disjointed and clumsy. When he finally rose to a sitting position it was hard to keep his back straight.

As sometimes happened during times of stress, his nose began to itch. When he reached up to scratch it, his breathing leveled off, and he suddenly found his own familiar, slightly nasal voice. Still not wanting to consider what was happing anything but conventional, he told himself that an intruder hid, if not in the room, then somewhere in the area.

"If someone is in here, you better get out!" he warned. "I've got a gun and…"

The distinct sound of gales of rich laughter tumbled through the portal and into the voice tunnel toward him. George sensed what was happening and thought, *Whoever it is certainly has a strange sense of humor.*

Again, the voice. "No one is here but you and me. And stop lying about having a gun."

A deep male baritone voice, observed George. *I'll play along with him. Maybe that will flush him out into the open.*

George reached back and held onto the side of the bed for balance. His legs felt like rubber, but he lurched forward anyway and made his way over to the window. His goal achieved, he parted the sheers and scanned the parking lot next to his building.

No one is out there. With a slight turn his head, he glanced back over one shoulder and surveyed the room. *I don't see anyone in here. Okay, I know what's happening. I've been working too hard. Time to take that dream vacation, spare no expense. Maybe go to London.*

"I order you to calm down!" Full of authority and confidence, the words surged through the portal, echoed in the voice tunnel like a loud rolling shout that left George wide-eyed, somewhere between terror and curiosity. It was warm in the room and his skin felt clammy, but he shivered as he felt a chill run up his back. His heart was beating faster and faster. His breathing was shallow and labored. Under other circumstances, he would have stopped dead in his tracks. But tonight, those words had the opposite effect. They jolted him into action.

Timid and shy by nature, the soft familiar lilt of his Jamaican accent was still distinct as he tried his best to control unfamiliar notes of hysteria forming in his throat. *I'm ready to explode, but what good would that do me? Got to get a hold of myself. Count to ten. Take a deep breath. It's going to be alright.*

That's what he told himself.

It didn't work.

I'm too wound up, need to move around. Frantic to be anywhere except where he was, George sprinted across the room toward his closet like a gazelle being chased by a lion. Thankfully he didn't crash into the mirror that hung on the closet door. For a long second, he stood motionless before it. He cocked his head first to the left, then to the right side as he gazed at the image that peered back at him, inspected it slowly from head to toe, searched for anything that might be unfamiliar or different.

The hairs on the back of his neck began to rise. What he saw in that mirror was only his own image. Even so, his skin tingled at the thought of something alien inside of him.

"Calm down?" he shouted. The sound ricocheted off the walls in the room like bullets. "Who cares what you want!" Then he added in a mocking voice, "Who, *what* the fuck are you and how did you get inside *my* head?"

Ra purposefully avoided taking the bait. *Perhaps I can reason with him, keep him calm.*

"To be correct," he asserted, "my essence is inside of your body. Where there was only one, now there are two, and the—

how did you put it? Oh, yes, tunneled voice coming through the ear inside of your head. That's my thoughts formed into words coming into your mind through a portal. Please allow me to explain. I come from Sun City, first plane capital of the Heavenly Realm to Earth on a mission. Since we're going to exist in close quarters for the time being, you may call me, Ra."

Stunned, George exploded, "What…who? Ra? That's it," he declared, as he stumbled back to his bed, lowered himself to the edge and sat down. Feet flat on the floor, he positioned himself so as not to fall off. It was his image in the mirror that hung on the closet door that stared back at him with pathetic-looking eyes. He rubbed his brow and thought, *That's what I get for burning the candle at both ends. As soon as the office opens, I'll call the travel agency and book the next flight to London.*

Chapter 29

Ra knew that being in George's body was the only way to appreciate the human experience. *Assault my essence? That's an understatement. This human has got my head spinning so fast, I'll probably never recover. I'm here now, so I'll have to make do. Nothing must interfere with my mission.*

"I know what you're planning," Ra barked, "and no, you won't book that flight to London. At least not until I leave. After that, you may do as you please."

George shrugged his shoulders, managed a dry swallow and asked, "Why me?"

"Why not?" Ra's words echoed through the voice tunnel then trailed off in a whisper. "Where I come from, we monitor the affairs of humanity. We understand things aren't going well, that some humans are not satisfied with conditions, and we'd like to help. That's why I was sent here. I need to borrow your body to let me experience what it's like to be in touch with your own and others feelings and emotions. By the way, you'll have to teach me how to do that."

"I, uh, have no idea what you're talking about. So you're holding my body hostage until you get what you're looking for?"

By this time, the conversation was becoming a bit more spontaneous. Carried by a deep chuckle, Ra's words flowed freely as they slid through the portal, down the tunnel, and landed in George's mind. "That's an interesting way of putting it. I was led to believe you might be one who is untouched. Tobias said I should learn from you."

"How do you know that name?"

I've got his attention, thought Ra.

"The Inner Council…Tobias, DaValla, and Julian. They are the ones who made the decision to involve you."

George riveted his gaze on the image in the mirror and asked, "So, Tobias sent you to be in my body? Did he tell you why he picked me?"

"Probably because you're a businessman—a lawyer, intelligent, good-natured, very humble about your achievements—and you consider yourself as ordinary. He's kept you informed about the tyrant, Karoon, and what's happening to deities in the Realm. If conditions on Earth are as they told me, then it's working with humans like you, those who sacrifice, reach back to help others in need with no thought of personal gain. That's how we'll make a difference. Teach me what you know so I can take it back to others. For a time there will be another being in your body, with its own personality. Please stop treating my presence as an intruder and fighting to expel me. I'm not the enemy. Reserve that for the satellite and those EMP's."

"Ok. I'll stick with my end of the deal, but it's almost like I have no choice. Do I have a choice?"

"There is always choice. However, understand that one way or another, my mission must be successful. I'll be the one to let you know when that happens. The fate of humanity and Sun City hangs in the balance."

"All right. Tobias didn't tell me there were any conditions. But, I'll still have some control over my own body…won't I?"

"Yes, there will always be give and take. Look on the bright side. Arrangements like this can be mutually rewarding. Perhaps I can help you achieve a goal. Maybe support you in some activity or…" Ra hesitated for a second, then added, "Help win the female of your dreams."

Help win the female of my dreams. That got George's attention. Sounded like Ra, or whatever he was, had experience in that area. Perhaps they could work something out. *My dream lover. If only…*

George reached into the odor processing center of his own brain, his olfactory bulb, pulled out part of a memory, and floated it through the portal and down the tunnel. Delicate, fragrant, warm plumeria mixed with subtle vanilla, heady and sensual, hit Ra, left him intoxicated as it teased him and mingled with his bright violet and lavender essence.

Ra had never been with a female. The only temptations he had ever succumbed to were fantasies, mental exercises of his own making. Now this body suit pulled him into its human experience like a whirlpool, made him experience what it was like to have a carnal craving born of human flesh.

He's testing me, thought Ra. *Tobias warned me not to become distracted.* Yet from the moment George sent the image of his dream lover through the portal, deep red swirled through the layers of his energy field. That stirred him, meant his innocence had already been violated.

Is this what I'm supposed to learn? He had to figure it out, keep things in proper perspective; otherwise, he would fail. And failure was not an option. Putting his essence into a container subject to self-consciousness was by definition intimate and risky. He had to remain focused, keep his energy field intact. Except for a specific reason. If he lost his focus, became distracted, then he would be useless to those back in Sun City who counted on him.

He was still reeling from the fragrance when George sent the full memory, an image of his dream lover—a woman with golden amber eyes and ruby red lips, tightly coiled jet black locks and long shapely legs.

Had he been back in Sun City, the burst of light red in his energy field would have been impossible to disguise. But this was planet Earth. He was in a human body suit and the only question on his mind was—who is Vera?

Chapter 30

Tick-tick-*tick*. George looked at the alarm clock on the nightstand beside his bed and hit the five-minute snooze button just as it was about to sound off. *Five thirty in the morning. Time to rise and shine. But I'm already awake. This Ra has cost me a good night's sleep.*

George took a deep breath and realized he had been sitting on the side of his bed for several minutes deciding whether to launch further protest. He not only thought about what Ra said, but how he said it. *Tobias. The mention of his name makes me want to verify this alien's true identity. Tobias is my friend but this one…I've got to be sure if what he says is a genuine plea or subtle deception. My life is going through a radical upheaval, and I've got to make sure it's for the right reasons. I think there's more to his story than what's being told.*

He clenched his fists, gritted his teeth, felt the muscles in his body tighten. *I've been so careful, more so than others in the underground. Could this be a dark worker? Are they on to me? Is this how they come for you?*

George steadied his nerves and held onto the side of the bed for balance. He had been sitting in the same position for so long that his legs felt numb, like pins and needles were sticking into them. Only after he tapped his heels several times on the floor did the feeling gradually subside. Finally able to rise to a standing position, he made his way over to the window and pulled one panel of sheers back to see the sky aflame with eastern morning sunlight—delicate shades of pink and orange heralding the arrival of the new day. Fingers of light had already made their way to the side of the building where his bedroom was.

As he stood there, his mind flooded with a tsunami of thoughts.

I've got to go on with my normal routine. I've got bills to pay. He had a heavy workload waiting for him at the office and hoped Ra's presence wouldn't complicate matters. That's what George thought, but he couldn't deny there was a part of him that welcomed a change in the all-too-predictable lifestyle he had become accustomed to. As far back as he could remember, there were daily routines and habits he faithfully followed. The time he dedicated to such pursuits was jealously guarded, starting with his morning ritual, which set the tone for the rest of his day. Wake up. Exercise. Shower. Dress. Eat breakfast. Leave for work. The same disciplined sequence, day after day, with little variation. In fact, he credited his acceptance of that kind of discipline with helping him finish law school and secure a top position as an attorney with one of the best full-service law firms in Kingston. Specializing in civil litigation, he built a solid reliable reputation and was on the fast track for consideration as managing partner.

Walking. Talking. Things like that he took for granted. He didn't think about the sequence of steps needed to perform those actions. They just happened. The same was true when it came to peace of mind. Like an impenetrable rock, it helped him remain calm and controlled, empowered him in his role as leader of the Jamaican underground movement. It kept him from losing his true self in all the madness that plagued Jamaica and the rest of the world. Tobias, his advisor and friend, never asked anything of him that conflicted with that desire. That's why he did not argue when Tobias said accepting Ra into his body was the right thing to do. It was just that now this thing was actually inside him. And, it was a little unsettling. *I must remember to accept the things I can't control.* But the echo of Ra's voice was still in his head and he thought, *This arrogant little ass! Who does he think he is? I'm not sure if I'm going to like this Ra fellow.* George felt the skin tighten around his eyes as one corner of his lip turned upward in a half-smile. *It's still my body and Ra has to understand he's just renting space in it.*

George stood there for a few seconds in the innocent warmth and pretended it came from Vera's' fingers as she caressed his body and invited him to…stay. But she wasn't there and he thought, *I suppose I should be grateful. At least I can have her with me in my dreams.*

Momentarily overcome by sadness, a tear made its way down one cheek. The track left a warm salty flavor that made his lips purse together as it slipped between the corners and into his mouth.

Beep-beep-*beep.* This time the sound was more insistent. Thankful for the extra time, George walked over, hit the stop button, then headed for the small bathroom. *A brisk three-minute cold shower, that's what I need. Nothing better to jump-start the day.* He adjusted the setting and stepped into the stall.

Over too soon, George stepped out onto a small rug. The EMP bracelet was worn at all times. The look of it was similar to leather bracelets commonly worn by men in the area, so it didn't stand out as unusual. A waterproof device, it didn't matter that he kept it on in the shower.

As he dried himself, he noticed that part of the temporary tattoo on his right forearm near his elbow had washed off. He had to be careful not let a few water drops put his independence and maybe his life, in jeopardy. *This is one thing I still have control over. Got to clean this up.* He reached inside the medicine cabinet for the stack of temporary decals discreetly hidden behind his cologne. He peeled one off and firmly held it until the image transferred to his skin. When finished, he stepped back and admired his work in the mirror that hung on the cabinet door.

Chapter 31

"You can't wear a short-sleeved shirt to work." The chastisement from Ra was unexpected.

"It's hot and humid, a typical clammy July day in Jamaica. I'll sweat to death in a long-sleeved shirt."

"A careless sunbeam will reveal traces of my own bright violet and lavender hues and cause your skin to have an unnatural shine to it. Someone might notice. If you don't believe me, stand by the window and look at your arm."

To prove his point, Ra had George move to the window, stand in the morning sunlight, noticing the difference for himself.

The bluish glow of his dark brown skin left no room for argument. "Oh, I see what you mean. Let's compromise. I'll wear a long-sleeved shirt to work. When I get off, there won't be much daylight left. I'll come back and change into a colorful guayabera short sleeved shirt, dark jeans and chinos. I'm taking us out for a tour of island life."

Now that some light filtered in, Ra convinced George to slow-down as he walked from the bedroom so he could help him better understand the space he lived in.

"What are we walking on?"

"Floors."

"What are they made of?"

"Wood, highly polished, and," George pointed to shelves along the walls filled with assorted linens and said, "Those are storage areas."

The closest room to the master bedroom was a small bedroom, windowless but cheerful. Furnished sparingly with a full-sized bed, there was also a one-drawer nightstand, and a six-drawer double dresser with an attached mirror.

"George, what's that covering the bed?"

"It's called a quilt. The color is mauve and the little designs are called floral medallions."

Next to that was a room used as a bathroom that featured a vanity-washstand combination and a soaking tub-shower combination. Ra asked George to step in and touch the top of the vanity-washstand combination.

"It's so smooth. What is the material called?"

"Marble. It has a cool feel to it."

"Yes, I sense it. It's pleasing."

A home office was set up in the next room. Complete with executive desk and chair, it housed a computer and wall unit that combined an interesting arrangement of closed drawers and open shelves crammed with a variety of books.

"Those are books. What are they about?"

"Mostly legal topics. Remember, I'm a lawyer by profession."

"Yes, I know."

The remainder of the condo was public space. Ra learned quickly, asking fewer and fewer questions as George moved through each room: a mud room that led to a back entry that also served as a laundry room; and an adjoining and well-fitted kitchenette that housed all the latest appliances.

A low, frosted glass room divider separated the kitchen from the dining room. Small yet formal, it boasted a candle-style chandelier suspended from the ceiling. If the sudden shower of bright orange that dappled Ra's energy field was any indication, then Ra's pleasure at what he witnessed was undeniable. *How grand it must make everything look when this light is turned-on, its long sweeping arms sending rays of shimmering beams reflected in the surface of that table with matching hutch filled with white china dishes, serving trays, and crystal glasses.* "What is the table made of?"

"Mahogany. It's been in my family for generations, so it's called an antique."

"Wonderful! Simply wonderful!"

The last room they came to was the living room. The furnishings had a rich feel to them that was sleek and polished, a perfect balance between the masculine and the exotic. A neutral color palate, accentuated with hues of rich purple, deep olive green, silver, and bright red served as a backdrop for pieces of wall art that reflected scenes of local Caribbean life.

Throw pillows were nestled in groups on a white sofa next to a matching armchair. A coffee table made from a small slab of petrified wood with a glass top cradled a smattering of carefully placed accessories chosen with conversation in mind. An entertainment center held a hodgepodge of audio and stereo equipment to include a large flat-screen TV and surround sound speakers. A well-stocked brass and glass contemporary minibar, complete with wine glasses, rounded out the story.

Ra didn't know why it happened, but suddenly he felt a scratchy sensation in his throat. Tears began to well-up in his eyes as he said,"A universe of space, a paradise with no one in it except yourself. Doesn't that bother you?"

"Sometimes," replied George. "But, I've become used to it. Besides, I need something—distractions—to take my mind off all the madness going on outside."

"Distractions? You *purposely* seek out distractions?"

"Yes. I call them mini-breaks. I never use distractions as an excuse to forget my responsibilities or the reality of the world I live in. But my mind is clearer when I take breaks, do or think about something else, even if just for a while. That helps me stay calm and better able to be in control of my emotions and feelings. Making my home as functional and comfortable as possible works for me, helps me achieve a certain peace-of-mind."

Chapter 32

The goal Tobias set for Ra was being fulfilled and in the most unlikely place possible—among humans in Jamaica.

Days became nights and nights became days until soon nearly one week had passed since their introduction.

George began to think of himself as more than Ra's teacher. He accepted Ra as the comrade he always wanted but never had. The very thought of the bond that formed between them caused a smile to spread across his mouth into his hazel brown eyes. *Finally, I have a close male friend, someone to just hang out with. I don't care how inexperienced he is, where he comes from, or that he's only in my body.*

As driven as he was to escape the cycle of poverty that limited others in his family, George also enjoyed the little things life had to offer. The peace-of-mind he found while decorating his home and doing good deeds for others made him happy. It relaxed him, lifted his spirit, helped him accept the things he couldn't control and deal with those he could.

George didn't know how long Ra would be in his body. But, he would do what he could to help him realize his goal. Learning how to be in touch with feelings and emotions was something that began with humans as infants. Ra was well past that stage. Beside his own body, he would use what the island had to offer: laid-back beaches, majestic waterfalls, lush landscapes and breathtaking sunsets, hustle and bustle, high-end boutiques, markets with souvenir stands. He would turn it all into one huge schoolhouse.

He knew that sensations conveyed through his connection with Ra caused certain basic physical reactions in Ra's body, either comfortable or uncomfortable. But, Ra needed to label the sensations without his help, then use that information to make decisions, like the purpose, when to control it or allow it to take full expression.

He would start with basic emotions like happy, sad, disgust, surprise, and pleasure.

To appreciate happy, George encouraged Ra to isolate the part of his own brain responsible for touch perception to savor the cool, smooth feel of leather bucket seats in his conservative black Toyota Cressida and the warm breeze playfully combing through his hair.

To show how two emotions could cause different feelings at the same time, George had Ra access the part of his brain that perceived sound to sense how listening to the beat of reggae tunes that blasted from the state-of-the-art sound system could make him feel happy but also sad if the volume hurt his ears because it was too loud.

They traveled roads, sometimes smooth and modern but more often nothing but red, rutted dirt defined by potholes. So, disgust was easy enough to identify by tapping into the part of his brain sensitive to movement through space.

They glided around the perimeter of the island, past baby-powder thick sand nestled at the foot of fishing villages; saw turquoise waves that crashed against rocky, coral-encrusted reefs. George drove with the windows down, inhaled deep breaths that sent waves careening into the pleasure center of his brain and also through the portal into Ra. Salted ocean air laced with whiffs of earthy, woody ganja that drifted down from plantations high in the misty Blue Mountains. The sweet smell of burning pimento wood used in shallow pits to smoke chicken, fish, and pork, mixed with the pungent aroma of exotic spies—garlic, ginger, thyme, cinnamon, nutmeg, and fiery Scotch bonnet peppers. The arrowhead warbler, Jamaican black bird, and the yellow-billed Amazon parrot— exotic birds whose distant cries greeted them as they motored down inland backroads that ran through tiny mountain hamlets past banana and coconut plantations—skirted mangrove swamps and rain forests, thick with fruit trees and orchids.

George even surprised Ra with an unscheduled trip to his favorite shoe shop—Donnie's Outlet. That was where he bought his Clarks. He and Ra were ideal shopping partners. Just to please Ra, George tried on almost every pair of shoes in his size in the place. Of course, Ra had an opinion about each pair he tried on. It amused George, reminded him of a fussy younger brother or *broda*, especially because Ra would never wear any of them himself.

Nighttime was reserved for social pursuits. The place to be was Spanish Town, capital and the largest town in the parish of St. Catherine, historic county of Middlesex. The crime capital of the Caribbean, Spanish Town was one of several places where the untouched could meet and greet without too much surveillance or interference.

George was very familiar with the area. He had been there many times over the years. His destination was always the same building hidden away on a seldom traveled backstreet. A lighted sign mounted on a tall, weathered post stood adjacent to a small parking lot next to the curb. There was only one word printed on the sign in tall, discernible calligraphy letters—Jolly's.

Chapter 33

To the casual observer, Jolly's was just an all-night joint, a lonely-hearts club. Frequented by those on the prowl for a lover or friend with benefits, it was a haven for spontaneous clandestine rendezvous by those who preferred to have their identities concealed and remain anonymous.

Ra would soon learn it was so much more.

As George became more comfortable with Ra's presence, he made him a party to information about the untouched and the resistance that would have been guarded from anyone else.

The first night George took his embedded guest to Jolly's, he parked in the small lot adjacent to the building, then began a short stroll down a meticulously maintained flagstone pathway flanked on either side by lush manicured tropical gardens, solar powered ground night lights, and a riot of majestic poinciana trees with beautiful canopies of red, fern-like flowers that reached out like umbrellas.

At the end of the pathway was a small courtyard and beyond that was an unexpected surprise—a scene best described as a combination of old-world colonial charm married with the crisp look so frequently associated with Caribbean ambiance.

The night air was hot, humid, and clammy. Even so, George took his time, allowed Ra to fully appreciate the charm of the three-story building's elegant Georgian architectural facade, modified to withstand the rigors of a tropical climate.

Then he went inside and lingered in the grand foyer. A fashion statement in relaxed formality, it welcomed guests with polished wooden floors that reflected a sheen in gold-trimmed wall mirrors. Rattan, bamboo, and woven furnishings sported plush velvet pillows with bold color palettes. The chandeliers were adorned with sparkling crystals and the windows with lush, hand-embroidered floor-to-ceiling drapes.

Dining rooms on either side of an ornate, curved mahogany staircase boasted high ceilings and palmetto fans, their rhythmic crackling sounds hardly noticeable above subdued but lively conversation. Square-shaped mahogany and walnut tables, neatly arranged in rows, accommodated anywhere from two to four guests each, offered candle light, crisp white linen, fine china, and crystal stemware.

An army of Jamaican workers, clad in black pants and starched, long-sleeved white shirts, moved in and out of the kitchen discreetly hidden behind an adjacent partition. Polite smiles and white-gloved hands offered menus that urged guests to choose a local staple like Ackee, curry chicken, or perhaps request a cooked-to-order specialty.

The second floor was only a few steps up the staircase. Once there, George walked through a small foyer adorned with floor-to-ceiling mirrors into a large room dominated by an ornate bar that spanned the entire length of one side. Floor-to-ceiling multi-paned windows left open on the other side let in a hot, humid July breeze.

Much less formal than the first floor, the atmosphere on the second floor was cool and casual. Cozy booths, ultra-seductive chaises and couches, leather-studded barstools…everything reflected the mellow hue of a mariner's palate of colors. Bar lights shimmered with soft flickers. Strategically spaced at intervals under the counter, each hit a huge beveled mirror on the wall at just the right angle to advertise a unique selection of top shelf local and world wine, spirit, and beer bottles.

As if that wasn't enough, the echo of live music floated down the staircase from the third floor, and provided the perfect backdrop for muted conversation in Jamaican patois held in cozy booths and secluded rooms suitable for more intimate activities.

With the exception of a small stage just large enough to hold a three-piece combo, a well-worn, sunken dance floor took up the entire area of the third floor. Each night it was crowded with dancers. Curves undulated. Breasts jiggled. Hips swayed. Men in long or short pants, flamboyant collared shirts and Clarks shoes; women in everything from dressy jeans to revealing thigh-high, low-cut, tight mini-skirts or dresses paired with spandex leggings. Subtle undertones of spice and sandalwood mixed with sweat and scented hair gel, floated in the air and through the huge French doors that opened onto the covered, open-air veranda and down into the courtyard below.

The final stop on the tour was the basement, where George lingered only for a few minutes, never long enough to raise questions in the minds of those who might notice his absence. Ra didn't understand why he went down there. The lighting was dim, and the place deserted. Honeycombed with corridors, he made it a point to walk up and down as many as possible. He tested the locks on concealed rooms, peeked into secret spaces, and sometimes carefully ran his hands along walls with surfaces that felt soft and made his skin itch.

"Disgusting! I don't like this feeling. Please stop." The urgency in Ra's voice was unmistakable. "It can't be good for your health. Why do you do it?"

"Don't worry," replied George. "I've done this many times. I don't like it, but it's necessary. My hands will get a good wash when I go upstairs. That's the feel of mineral wool. It's a special type of insulation that has lead particles. I'm checking to see that it's still in place."

"You don't let your dislike get in the way of what needs to be done."

"Exactly."

When satisfied, George stopped by the restroom, then made his way back upstairs to join the activities in progress. The first thing he did was look for familiar faces in the crowd. Not finding any, he went on to the second floor and into the bar room. He stood at the top of the stairs for a moment, long enough to let Ra take everything in.

A long whistle, barely audible, followed by a guarded but undeniably happy chuckle, tumbled back at him through the ear inside of his head. "Not bad, human, not bad!" Ra's words said it all.

Not particularly hungry or ready to break out into a hot, clammy sweat, George thought, *Tonight I'll spend most of my time in the bar on the second floor.* Flooded with soft coral ambient lighting, the room was just dark enough to be the perfect place for a human with secrets to keep.

As fortune would have it, there was an unoccupied couch near the bar positioned in just the right spot with a good view of the entire room. No sooner had George nestled in when the sound of a familiar male voice with a cheerful yet professional lilt caused him to lift his gaze to survey the face of the speaker.

"May I take your order, sir?"

I know it's dark in here, thought George, *but you should recognize one of your regulars.*

"Hello, Tony. How's it going tonight?"

"Oh, Mr. Patel, it's you. I almost didn't recognize you. It's so dark in here. Nice seeing you again, sir."

George smiled and sent a message through the portal. *Tony's one of us.*

"Tony, I'll have a dirty martini, stirred, not shaken, please."

"Very well, sir." Then he pivoted on one foot and quickly made his way back toward the bar, only to return shortly with the order. As he reached down to put the glass on the table, George caught a glimpse of part of a tattoo on his right forearm near his elbow. The shape of a feather with the hollow shaft pointing upward was all too visible.

George motioned to Tony to come closer, then whispered, "You might want to roll your sleeve down to obscure that tattoo from view."

"Thank you, Mr. Patel."

With that George reached into the inside pocket of his jacket, retrieved one of his own sanctioned ostrich feather shaft pointing downward decals, and, together with a twenty-dollar bill, handed it to Tony.

"Thank you, Mr. Patel!" The gesture (and generous tip) brought a broad smile to the young man's lips. He pocketed his reward and scurried to another table, but not before he turned and said, "Thank you, sir!"

Even with fans running, the air in the place was humid and hot. George nursed his drink, anxious to see how Ra reacted to the exotic concoction.

"What is this?"

"Alcohol. Gin and vermouth mixed with olive juice."

"Strange, it's…ha,…ha…I'm spinning.It's so pleasurable, almost…

George laughed softly. *Now it's my turn to glimpse your world,* he thought as impressions floated into his mind. Bubbles of soft yellow, splashes of glittery pink taking shape and form as hazel eyes, curvaceous breasts, a slim waste, skin the color of ochre, a little golden comb holding back coarse, jet-black hair, luscious lips…all mingled within layers of rich, magnificent bright violet and lavender hues…vibes, female and male…melding into one beautiful kaleidoscopic explosion.

Impressed by the newly emerging erotic imagination of his visitor, George wondered, *who is this beauty?*

The experience had curiously stirred feelings within him, made him anxious to be on the prowl. As he sipped his dirty martini, George took inventory of the women present. *Tall. Short. Thin. Plump. All eye candy. Very nice, but tonight I'm looking for you—again.*

That's when he saw *her*—again—lounged on a leather stool, all alone at one end of the bar.

George fixed his gaze on her. *Hello, my darling, my soul, my love. Now you're even in my dreams, and you always look so beautiful, like you just stepped out of a high-fashion magazine ad.* Intrigued by the vision that was her, he squinted his eyes in the dim light and thought, *You literally take my breath away!*

Lup-*dup*. Lup-*dup*. George's heart beat quickened and the swish of his breath got faster.

"What's happening George?"

"The same thing that happened to you when you thought about that beauty with all the bubbles. You said you wanted to experience connections, what it's like to be in touch with your own and others' feelings and emotions. I'm going to show you how it feels to connect with your heart. It's called intimacy and you're about to get your first lesson."

The first thing about her that caught George's attention was the mane of tightly coiled, jet-black locks that fell slightly below her shoulders, each one sporting a delicate golden bead. The way the light played off those beads brought a faint smile to his lips and made him wonder if she had been one of those little girls he sometimes watched teasing little boys with their bouncy plats.

Then he contemplated the sensuous curve of her calf muscles, accentuated by the way she held her long, shapely legs, first crossed then relaxed, one leg on top of the other. Each time the thigh-high hemline of the black silk dress she wore shifted, it relaxed him, reminded him of the steady ebb and flow of how waves played with sand at Hellshire Beach.

Even though the traffic at the other end of the bar was busy, she commanded more than her fair share of attention from the male staff behind the counter.

She's in her usual place, a venue regular, noted George.

One worker behind the bar called-out a name—Vera. She turned to face him, beamed him a radiant smile.

Now I have a name to go with that lovely face. Vera. It means truth, exactly what I need more of in my life. Is it just a trick of the lighting, or did she glance my way?

"You mean, our way, don't you?" Teasing as his tone was, Ra's comment wasn't appreciated.

George never suspected anything would challenge his promise to be Ra's teacher. But that comment annoyed him. *He's just being childish. I'm the adult in the room, so I've got to remain objective.* He decided to laugh it off and sent a reply back through the portal to Ra. *In your dreams, young virgin, Inna…yuh…dreams.*

George watched Vera as she dined alfresco from a small plate on the counter slathered with jerk chicken nachos. It drove him crazy to see the way she slowly nudged sticky bits around her plate with perfectly polished, fire-engine red nails, scooped them up to pause before her ruby red lips, eagerly devoured them, then daintily ran her tongue across her lips and sucked her fingers clean.

He prided himself on self-control; but tonight, as he watched her chew, he could almost taste the spicy flavor as it washed over her tongue.

The thoughts that tumbled through the portal in his mind. Was it his imagination running wild? The voice was low, deep, and raspy, so he knew it wasn't Ra. *You would give anything to be that tongue. You would do everything to her with your tongue.*

Chapter 34

All the while George fought a losing battle with himself to keep passion from growing into lust. I don't want it to be like that with her. I want to get to know her first, maybe start with dinner, just the two of us. See where things go.

Lost in the contemplation of the sweetness of romantic intimacy, it took several seconds before he acknowledged Tony, the young waiter, standing patiently before him. His glass was almost empty. With a wave of his hand, he dismissed Tony and thought, It's now or never. He rose and, with his glass in hand, casually strolled over to the bar and slid his body onto the stool next to Vera.

George inhaled deeply and thought, Her fragrance is honey sweet like the delicate floral scent of warm plumeria mixed with subtle, sensual vanilla. Just like in my dream.

In one smooth motion, he reached into the inside pocket of his jacket, pulled out a fifty-dollar bill, and casually plopped it on the counter in front of the bartender. Still holding his half-empty glass, he swirled the remains of his dirty martini around, gestured to the bartender and said, "I'll have another one of these. Keep the change, and give the lady another one of whatever she's drinking."

The lighting at the bar was much brighter. Just for a second, when Vera flashed him a tight-lipped smile, George thought he saw a glint of satisfaction in her golden amber eyes.

The corners of her lips moved up just a bit as she avoided his gaze. "Thanks, I'm drinking a Cosmo…Caribbean Cosmopolitan."

A fruity taste, George thought, that will sweeten your lips—for me. He leaned close to Vera as though they were already a couple. "Excuse me," he murmured. "My name is George Patel. May I ask you a question?"

Vera picked up the cocktail napkin next to her plate and daintily dabbed at the corners of her mouth before answering.

"You may," she purred, "and I might answer."

"This is my first time here and…"

George, shame on you for lying like that. George recognized the sound chastisement accompanied by gales of laughter as that of the voice of the alien within him.

Objectivity aside, he felt his patience being tested. He laughed and replied, *shut up, young virgin. Or I'll find a way to shut that portal down!* Delivered with a touch of humor, the thinly veiled threat was more than enough to let Ra know his commentary was unwanted.

"I'm having difficulty deciding what to order. I can't help but notice you've chosen one of my favorite dishes, jerk chicken. Everything on the menu looks so good. Would you recommend—"

Before he could finish his sentence, Vera picked up her fork, scooped a bite from her plate, then moved it slowly toward his mouth.

"You be the judge."

Pungent aromas—allspice, thyme, scotch bonnet—floated across the fork into his nostrils. George thought he opened his mouth wide enough, but he miscalculated, which left a small bit on one side.

Vera giggled, folded her napkin until only an unused corner was visible, then reached over toward George and gently patted the offender away.

As she drew back her hand, George reached out, felt the warmth of her smooth, dark brown skin as he caught her hand gently in his. She didn't resist as his thumb caressed the back of her hand, then slipped over to her palm where it found a sensitive spot…pressed…then released.

George's dream had finally come true. Each night for the next week they met at Jolly's. Cocktails. Dinner. Conversation turned one-way by Vera, always about George's interests and habits. And, if she probed too deeply, a skillful shift of topic by George to something less intrusive…perhaps an invitation to grove to the beat of the reggae rhythm. *Dum-bum-bum, dum-bum* on the dance floor until the last call and the place shut down in the wee hours of the morning.

On the eighth night, George found himself waiting for her at the bar on the second floor. Instead of eating downstairs, he planned an intimate dinner for two in one of the secluded rooms away from the view of bar patrons.

It's time we got to know each other better, he concluded.

The evening crowd was filing in as he searched faces with the thought of sweet things to come.

Chapter 35

Things were going much better than expected. Ra enjoyed how George watched over him and sensed he sincerely wanted to help his mission be successful. The only time he had ever felt that way was back in Sun City with Tobias.

There was an innocence about George that resonated with Ra since both of them came from places defined by chaos and selfishness. George became the very definition of what it meant to be human. Through him, Ra began to understand how to connect with his own and other's feelings and emotions to get the peace-of-mind he needed to cope with stressful situations and stay grounded.

Ra knew that George's vibe was now his vibe. But it could never be achieved without free will. George fought hard to keep it the way. Ra would do the same.

So it confused him when George put all that he was in jeopardy, when he began to act in a way that seemed to go against the vibe he resonated to.

Vera. It was all because of Vera.

Ra remembered Tobias' warning not to give in to temptation. And he would have been a liar to deny his anticipation of pleasuring Vera, if only vicariously through George. But this night there was something about her he found unsettling. Whatever it was, it was strong and troubled him.

"George, be careful. I—"

You don't know what you're talking about!

That didn't sound like the George he had come to know. The sharp words surprised him, sent the tunnel ringing like a bell.

Still Ra persisted.

"Please, think about it. Why do you only meet at the club, where shadows play with dim light and obscure what needs to be clearly seen: whether the shaft of the ostrich feather tattooed on her right forearm points up or down?"

Just…be still!

It didn't matter what he cautioned. George was hooked.

"All right George, if that's the way you want it." The portal inside George's head vibrated with the echo of a deep breath exhaled in one long, loud snort of resignation.

Chapter 36

No sooner had Vera walked into the foyer than she started thinking about George. She remembered the night they met, how she felt when he claimed the bar stool beside her and offered to buy her a drink. She'd noticed him before, but didn't want to mess things up by approaching him. Being too pushy might scare him off. After all, he was her prey.

But the change in him that night confirmed that her mojo was still working. *He's finally worked up enough nerve to talk to me. Now that I see him up close, he's a real looker. Strange, but I thought his eyes were a different color. Maybe it's the lighting in here. He's acting like an entirely different person, not the shy little man with a soft, slightly nasal voice, always sitting alone on that couch. I like the change.* It was the moment she had hoped for, an opportunity to lure him in, disarm him, mesmerize him so he would think and do what she wanted…tell her all his secrets.

She smiled demurely and thought, *He's mine. Anwir will be pleased.*

Already running late, she began studying her image in the floor-to-ceiling mirrors that adorned the walls, then complimented herself with a pleased smile and a question, *who are you?* A familiar voice, her mother's voice, reached out from the past to answer her. Sugary sweet, desperate to live her own spoiled life through her daughter, it whispered, *"You're mi Vera."*

I am my muma's creation, Vera declared. The muscles around her mouth relaxed, and the chill in her golden amber eyes warmed as she reminded herself, *I can't let my true intentions show in my face. But he's starting to get to me. The way he walks, talks…smells. He really turns me on. I like him just a little too much. If things were different, I could…but that's not how it is.*

With that, she adjusted her makeup, then wiggled her way across the room to George.

Tied with a single string that looped around her neck, she was dressed in a red, off-the-shoulder, chiffon, halter dress with a ruffled hemline that hugged her body in all the right places. A long, red silk scarf, secured by a little gold clasp, added a touch of sophistication as it hung low enough to cover her right forearm. Red high heels clicked. Red handbag swung from one shoulder by a gold chain.

A living, breathing, dangerous seductive knockout. If she had misgivings, they would have to be pushed aside. There was work to be done. And a severe penalty for failure.

Chapter 37

Seated on a stool, George leaned his back against the bar. He aimed for that cool, calm vibe women so often found attractive.

Vera was late, and his imagination was running wild. *Was she in an accident? Did she stand me up? Maybe I should call the police.*

Just as he was about to lose it, he spotted her as she pushed her way through the crowd. He rushed over and met her relaxed stroll half-way.

"Hello, beautiful, I've been waiting for you." His hazel-brown eyes sparkled as he bent down and gave her a quick, light kiss on the check.

"Sorry to be late, dear." Vera flashed him a little smile, but her jaw tightened as she avoided his gaze. "It took a while for the taxi to come, and I had some business to take care of."

George was so crazy about her that he didn't belabor the subject. "No problem. I've got a space for us right over here."

He reached for Vera's hand and held it confidently as they made their way around patrons settled in for the evening. Just a few steps away, an oversized booth and a table in a secluded room awaited their arrival. Already set with service ware, the table was strewn with flower petals and boasted tapered candles. An electronic pager, placed discreetly near the table, would assure their privacy until they were ready to leave.

"Come, sit down." George waited until Vera was seated, then slid in beside her.

When a young waiter appeared, George regarded him for a second, then inquired, "Tony's not on duty tonight?"

"No, sir, it's his night off. My name is Lloyd. I'll be serving you this evening."

"Very well."

Lloyd handed them menus and waited silently with pad and pencil in hand.

A basic briefing from Anwir had alerted Vera about what to look for that might reveal the identity of untouched humans, like EMP bracelets or pendants. Even in the dim lighting, a fleeting glance confirmed that George wore one of the bracelets. Vera filed the information for later as she made her selection from the menu.

"I'll have broiled lobster and macaroni salad."

After a few seconds, George piped, "The barrel-roasted chicken in mountain mango chutney for me."

Lloyd made a few notes on his pad, then inquired, "And, to drink?"

"A Cosmo…Caribbean Cosmopolitan, for the lady. I'll have a dirty martini, stirred, not shaken. But we'll start with two glasses of ice-cold water. It's so hot tonight."

"That it is, sir."

When the food came, it was quickly eaten. Afterwards they sat there, side by side, and sipped their drinks in silence.

"George, I—"

"Don't. Not tonight. Let's just…"

The hour was late, and that, along with a full stomach and the flicker of candlelight, should have made him sleepy. Instead, George felt like he was on an adrenalin high. He gazed at Vera. What he wanted from her was more than a quick fuck.

Passion, the kind that came with love, the prospect of a future together. That's what he wanted. That's what he needed. That's what he planned to tell her.

But the feeling that suddenly engulfed him was lust, pure and simple.

Ra! This must be your doing.

"No, George. It's not me, but I'm willing to come along for the ride!"

George couldn't control it. Both he and Ra were now passengers in his body. With only the dim flicker of waning candlelight as witness, he put one arm around Vera, pulled her close.

Her startled glance betrayed that she hadn't quite been expecting so direct an approach. But she didn't resist him and came closer. He lifted her chin, then their lips met and they kissed until they were both breathless. She reached for him and the click-*clack* sound of her fire-engine red fingernails as they undid each button, then opened his shirt excited George. The touch of her hands, soft and warm as they ran across his chest, played with his nips, made them rock hard, drove him crazy. Then, as her hands wandered lower, unzipped his pants, explored his cock with an unexpected familiarity, his fingers reached under her dress, found her thighs, stroked the satin smoothness of her skin, ventured higher past her lacy silk thong until they reached the bristles of her neatly trimmed bush, then rubbed her moist slit up and down, side to side.

When she moaned, "It's so hot in here," George gallantly reached over and dipped his fingers in his water glass, wet them with a few drops, hoped it would please her to feel the coolness on her skin. In his haste, he accidentally splashed some on his decal. What should have remained intact washed away. But he was too preoccupied to notice.

George reached up, carefully removed the long, red silk scarf, and untied the single string that looped around Vera's neck. When her halter top dropped to her lap, he reached out, cupped first one breast then the other with his free hand, bent down and ran the tip of his tongue in circles around her nipples. *Sweet like honey.* He carefully pressed her down on the bench, felt her reach for him as he entered her, felt her body arch toward him as his pressed down on hers.

Odd that at a time like this George's thoughts would turn to soft yellow bubbles, splashes of glittery pink taking shape and form as hazel eyes, curvaceous breasts, a slim waste, skin the color of ochre, a little golden comb holding back coarse, jet-black hair, luscious lips.

"George…*George*? Your fingers…why are they so… cold?"

"Say my name, baby…say my name." No longer the soft, slightly nasal lilt that was his own voice, George's tone was suddenly deep, resonant, almost sultry.

Ra? Get out of here, George ordered. *Vera's mine.*

The portal began to close but not before a different voice—low, deep, and raspy—echoed through the ear in George's head. Neither George or Ra, it gloated with sarcasm. Only heard by Ra, it gave him a reminder that was quite clear and concise. "Sprite, I promised that if you played your cards right I'd enlighten you about enjoying the affection of a scantily clad female. Well, I *always* keep my promises."

Pressure. Warmth. Wetness. Vibrations shooting up and down George's spine…*and also Ra's spine.*

Sweet moment of climax, too soon passed. Was it two, or maybe more, that came together as one?

Chapter 38

It was almost dawn. George called a taxi for Vera, paid the driver in advance, and waved goodbye.

As they rounded the corner from Jolly's, Vera leaned over and gave the driver an address different than the one she gave while in George's presence. The next time they stopped was at her apartment in Trench Town, about thirty miles from Spanish Town.

Vera walked inside and turned on the lights. Her place was on the ground floor of a two-story unit. Just a one-bedroom studio with a bath and small kitchenette. The water was hot, the plumbing worked, and the landlord kept the rat population controlled.

Her first stop was the bedroom. Undoing the string that looped around her neck, Vera let her dress fall to the floor. Thankful it wasn't too wrinkled from lying in the booth with George, she picked it up and hung it behind the bathroom door on a rack beside her robe, then slipped out of her bra and panties and walked to the shower. As she turned the setting to warm and stepped into the stall, she thought, *It was hot in that place. I can't understand how his fingers could be so cold. A hot shower is just what I need.*

How she loved hot showers. A chrome-framed caddy hung from a small hook pushed into a seam in the grout of the wall. It had two levels. The lower glass shelf was a sloppy, soapy mess, complete with a tattered washcloth that had seen better days. The top glass shelf was neater. That's where she kept her loofa sponge and body wash. *Coffee and Coconut or Rose Water? I'm gonna go with…Coffee and Coconut.*

Carefully pouring a small amount into her hands, she splashed it on her body, starting with her shoulders. She enjoyed the coarse, brittle feel of the loofa sponge as it moved across her collarbone, but she discontinued the abrasive strokes just shy of her breasts. There she preferred to use her hands to gently cup each one while her fingers moved round and round, traced the outlines of each areola, massaged each nipple until it became sensitive and swollen. That brought back thoughts of her night at Jolly's with George. *I can't get over the change in him…the smell of his cologne. Wasn't it Atelier Pomelo Paradis? Yes. I can still smell it all over my body.*

Rinsing the foamy lather from her skin, she loved how it caressed every curve, left a residual coating that felt like silk sheets, slippery and smooth. Reluctantly she turned off the water, stepped out onto a small bath rug and dried herself. The bathroom was steamy, and as she wiped away the mist that fogged on the mirror that hung on the medicine cabinet door, the image of a permanent tattoo on her forearm became visible—a feather with its shaft pointed down.

For a moment, she thought of her mother. *"There you are. That's mi Vera."* Her mother used to say that to her as she groomed her to fulfill her own unrealized dreams. Crime. Ghettoes. Poverty. Drugs. Working as a maid in the homes of well-to-do folks. Living off meager wages and tips. *"You're gonna move up in life, Vera. The 'she goddess' in mi Vera deserves better than this. Make your muma proud."*

Early in life, Vera vowed poverty wasn't in her future. Not if she could help it. The question was, how low was she willing to go? She schemed and plotted, told herself that she wasn't a bad person, did anything and everything until a lucky break brought her to the attention of humans under the control of dark workers…and Anwir. Her willingness to use her obvious physical attributes endeared her to them. That would be her ticket out. Her goal in life was to become one of them, and when the opportunity for service arose, her name was first on their list.

Her bathroom ritual completed, Vera wrapped herself in her robe. Happy to be warm and comfortable, she walked back into her bedroom and sat on the side of her bed. She didn't even flinch at the sound of the low, deep, raspy voice that echoed through the portal in her mind.

"Vera…What's the status?"

"Good news, Anwir. All has gone as planned. I met him at Jolly's last night and…"

"Excellent. We've had that place under surveillance for years. We suspect it's a meeting place for the untouched. The lighting in there is so dim. We can't say for sure, but we have a hunch the human body suit you were with, George Patel, is involved. We've tried sending EMP's out at different times of the day and night, but somehow, they've figured out our event schedules. I, uh, that is to say, we know that someone up here in Sun City is warning humans just before an EMP is sent, maybe using a sound or a light. That gives them time to protect themselves, but if they are preoccupied, well, that's when we get them. There was another EMP event last night, and if any of them were caught off guard…let's just say they're normalized by now. Did you get a look at the human's forearm?"

"Uh, no, he resisted and the light was dim, but …," She paused, startled by how her thoughts suddenly drifted to the way George gazed at her with smoldering eyes. Were they hazel brown or emerald green? Suddenly, she couldn't remember. George was untouched. That she knew for sure. Overcome by an unfamiliar pang of guilt, she thought, *How can I take pride in betraying a good man whose only sin is wanting to control his own life? What happened between us...was it carnal sex or maybe something more?* It made her feel lightheaded, magnified the lup-*dup* sound of her own heartbeat in her head. Her golden amber eyes clouded with confusion. And regret. How low could she go? That was no longer a mystery.

Disgusted with herself, one corner of her mouth lifted slightly as she replied stiffly, "I kept him occupied. He arranged an intimate dinner in one of the secluded rooms on the second floor not far from the bar. I'm sure he had no idea that an electronic pager was next to the table. I kept his mind on other things. You should have been there." The tactful omission of the bracelet he wore and the false tattoo were the least she could do to keep George safe.

"Yes, I can imagine how entertaining the experience was for all involved. By the way, I'll put in a good word about you with Karoon. It's not every human female that can deal with ménage à trois."

Vera's face paled. Thinking she misheard him, she asked, "What's that?"

"I'm sure you noticed the difference in the human—the way he came on to you, how he, uh, performed in that booth?"

"Maybe, but—"

"You never know who might come through when a portal opens. Your George has been the willing body suit for a hotshot deity named Ra. Karoon sent him down to Earth to be an observer, discover the identity of the leader of the untouched and how they protect themselves from being normalized, report back to him so he could fix the problem. I hope he did, but even if he didn't..." Gales of laughter careened through the portal, then, in his low, deep, raspy voice, Anwir continued, "Thanks to you, it's possible Ra got normalized."

"But, I thought you told me a deity couldn't be normalized."

"That's what we thought, but if an outside force intervened, distracted him, kept him from keeping his energy field intact."

"Then he experienced everything George felt and *did*?" Vera's voice deteriorated into a strangled moan.

"Ah, yes." Anwir's voice took on a tone that was cold and unapologetic. "Something else happened that could never be done in the Realm. Let me be the first to congratulate you. It's still early, but there's a little one on the way. Evidently, Ra also found you desirable. You see, male sterility runs in George's family. George will be the child's human father in name only. We'll keep this between us. There's no need for George to find out. Human males are so sensitive about matters of this nature. That brings me to my next point."

Still reeling from the revelation, Vera stammered, "Which is ?"

We…that is to say, Karoon, Isfet, and myself, agree that you should find a way to get George to—what do you humans call it? Marry you. That way, we can keep an eye on him and the child. The true father being a deity, and you being, well…because it happened while he was inside George, we're anxious to see if the child is untouched or normalized. That can only be detected as time goes by. Look on the bright side. You'll make your mumas' dreams for you come true."

"What the f—." Vera never completed her sentence. She stilled her voice as she remembered who Anwir was and what he could do to her. Backed into a corner of her own making, she shrugged and said, "It's my honor to be of service. Oh, there is one thing."

"What's that?"

"Well, while I was keeping George…uh, Ra…uh, whoever occupied, he kept talking about yellow and pink bubbles.

Anwir had no love for Ra. Hell, he didn't even like him. When he saw a chance to discredit him, he eagerly took advantage of it. He opened another portal between himself and Ra, then sent a message that was built on a lie.

Karoon says you've served your purpose. There's no need for you to remain on Earth. Vacate the body suit. Return to the Realm at once with what you've learned.

Chapter 39

It was just past dawn when George arrived back at his condo in Mona Heights. He made a beeline for his bedroom, hoping to catch a few hours of sleep before going to work. His head hit the pillow, and just as he was about to drift off, an all-too-familiar baritone voice floated through the portal into his mind.

"George, I have something to tell you."

"Not now, please. I'm so sleepy."

Unfortunately, the sound of his tired voice didn't stop Ra from continuing.

"George, please wake up and listen. I've got to go back to Sun City."

George sat up, then turned to sit on the side of the bed. *I was just getting accustomed to having you around.* He cleared his throat, and when he spoke, the soft lilt in his voice had a somber edge.

"What? You can't leave now. I don't understand. Why do you have to go back so soon?" George searched for some meaning as to why his life was being turned upside down for a second time.

"Because my mission is complete, or so I've been informed by others."

George didn't know why it happened, but for some reason his gaze wandered across the room to the open closet door where it settled on his shoes. He was so particular about the condition of those shoes. He had a closet full of designer shoes, casual shoes, sneakers and sandals. His Clarks— genuine leather Jamaican boots—were his trophies. All expensive, all name brands, some dated, some still in style. Each pair spit-polished clean and kept in pristine condition.

So many quality pairs of shoes. They fit the image of what the outside world expected him to wear. But of all his shoes, the ones he loved best were a pair of well-worn slippers he kept in the foyer next to the front door.

At the end of each hard day at work, he took off the mask he showed to the world. When he stepped across the threshold of his front door into his home, there was no better stress buster than to slip his bare feet into those comfortable old slippers. The soft leather lining conformed to the curves of his feet, made him imagine what it must feel like to walk among the clouds.

No matter how hard he tried, no matter how good his hygiene was, at the end of the work day his feet were always a little sweaty and stinky. But those slippers never complained. He took care of them, and like old friends, they never judged him. They gave him permission to show his true self, the part of him that would always remember the good and the bad of the struggle it took to step up in life.

He was always driven by his own purpose, and his own purpose was to be a man of the people. He wasn't born with a silver spoon in his mouth. His parents and their parents before them had been farmers living in the rural areas of Jamaica. They struggled to put food on the table, but never turned anyone away from their door who was truly in need.

Never alone, he was always lonely. A lonely child with no time for playmates. A lonely adult with no opportunity to experience the emotional satisfaction that came with having close male friends to swap stories with, process world events, brag about achievements, vent about defeats. Living with loneliness was justified by a promise to break a generational cycle. His parents always told him he would be the one to make it happen. He never doubted, and so it did when he became one of the top attorneys on the island. Now he lived a simple but comfortable life. Still, he never forgot where he came from, always tried to reach back and give a hand up to those in need. Service to others over self-interest. There would always be women; but like a comfortable pair of old slippers, a good male friend was hard to find.

The lilt of George's Jamaican accent was almost lost in the soft tone of his voice. "You said you would stay until you accomplished your mission. Did you learn the secret…find what you were looking for?"

"There are some things I want—*need* to tell you. It all started when I answered an ad for a position as a Creator God Apprentice under the direct supervision of Karoon, the tyrant. I didn't know much about his treachery at the time, so I admired him, put my trust in him, wanted my vibe to be just like his. He sent me to your planet to monitor the affairs of humanity, find out who leads the resistance against him and why. But being here…well, I've come to seriously regret that decision. I'm sure that mission wasn't meant to insure your well-being."

"Karoon already rules Sun City with an iron fist and a sly tongue that's caused a rift between the light and dark workers who exist in that place. He claims he created your planet and humans and, in the beginning, loved your kind. But his love was conditional. Now, he's angry because humanity rejected his control and desire for worship. His anger is so great that he would find a way to make you conform or punish you, take away all that makes your life worth living, just as he has tried to do with deities.

"The truth is that I had conflicting feelings about coming to Earth. Karoon told me that humans were worthless and I believed him. Until I came here and met you. I've looked within your essence, learned the truth of who you are. You've always been concerned with the welfare of others. Unconditional love, isn't that what you call it? The way you came to accept my presence, share your body with me, help me understand the best and worst of what it is to be human. Except for a very few deities like Tobias, that's the exception where I come from."

George felt the muscles in his own throat tighten as Ra's deep, resonant baritone voice became noticeably unsteady.

"No one except Tobias thought I would amount to anything. But Tobias made me *believe* I had something to contribute that no one else could. Service to others over self-interest. That's what coming of age rituals are all about. But the next one was months away. He wanted me to do something right now that I didn't feel qualified to do. My only concern was for my vibe, for pleasure, adventure, and excitement. My reluctance shamed me."

George hesitated, then said, "Ra, I'm glad you realize that humans and deities aren't that different when it comes to feelings and emotions."

"That's true. Humans who are normalized have it in them to do good deeds but don't because they are controlled by an outside force. Feelings and emotions haven't abandoned deities in the Heavenly Realm. It's just that light workers are punished for open and honest emotional displays in front of those in power. They're out of practice, so they don't remember how to be in touch to make thoughts real, let alone manage them or use them to make wise decisions. Tobias told me that I didn't know who I was or what I wanted. He was correct, but through you, I've experienced new vibes—courage, peace-of-mind, intimacy. That's the secret I was looking for. You've taught me how to bridge the divide."

George listened intently to Ra's words. As the muscles in his throat began to relax, he asked, "What will happen when you return to Sun City?"

"Tobias reminded me that decisions have consequences. He's known Karoon much longer than I have, and he asked me a simple question—how I wanted to be remembered—as the one who made a difference or as Karoon's legacy. What I've learned from you has helped me answer that question.

"I'll tame the desires within me because they are like beasts. I'll use what I learn to help me step into my power and claim it. I have never been clearer about what my true calling is. To teach light workers, show them what I learned, hopefully rekindle their knowledge of who made them and how special their gifts are. Yes, that's my destiny, to trigger what has laid dormant for so long.

"Tobias will be anxious to add what I've discovered to our information bank. I'll find a way to meet with him privately. Karoon and his minions have done enough damage to my home and your planet. With our efforts united against him, we will end this tyrant's reign of terror. We'll take care of things on our end, find a way to stop those EMP shockwaves, and do what we can to protect you. As it is in Sun City, I suspect he has spies here among humans. After last night—you won't like what I'm going to say, but be careful of Vera."

"I'm going to ask her to marry me."

"Well then," Ra replied, in a voice that was uncharacteristically flat and toneless, "congratulations are in order."

"Do you think we'll ever meet again?"

"Anything is possible."

"There's just one request I have before you go. Ra, show me the *real* you, what you really look like."

"Are you sure?"

"Yes."

"Every being vibrates with a particular level of energy, which is used to categorize them into any one of seven planes in what you call the universe. The first plane is where Sun City, capital of the Heavenly Realm is. Humans are fourth plane beings. I'm a sprite, the youngest in my colony. Soon I will be afforded full status as a second plane deity at the coming-of-age ritual. I can take any form I want, but what I'm going to show you is my true self, and how I want you to remember me."

A shapeless cloud of energy with rich layers of bright violet, boiling, flashing, swirling in and out, round and round. Within it a male form took shape. Well over six feet tall, with emerald green, almond-shaped eyes, jet-black coils, beard shaped into a perfect curve at his cheeks and square jawline, creamy golden-brown skin touched by a lavender blush.

Stunned, George was speechless for a long second. Then he nodded his head in approval and said, "I've always had a fondness for the color purple."

With that, his body relaxed. Ra closed the portal between them and went back the way he came…a bright flash of light, violet and lavender, that slipped quietly into the morning dawn.

Part 3 - Maat

Chapter 40

Ra had mixed feelings about being back in Sun City. Duty and obligation dictated that he return as ordered by Karoon, but he missed George, the human who he now called friend.

Thoughts of George and Jamaica were on his mind as he walked through the lobby of The Court and heard a familiar smooth, deep, velvety baritone voice call his name.

"Ra, is that you?"

"Wah gwaan. Hello Tobias." Ra smiled and nodded in greeting. I've just returned from Jamaica. I have so much to tell you and—"

Tobias cut him off mid sentence. "*Wah* what? Never mind. What are you doing back here so soon?"

"Soon? I received Anwir's message that I was to return, that I had served my purpose on Earth in the human body suit. He said the order came directly from Karoon."

"As far as I know, Karoon sent no such message. I wonder what Anwir is up to?"

As if on cue, Anwir walked in from the other side of the lobby. He spotted Ra and Tobias and tried to turn around before they noticed. But he wasn't quick enough.

"Shh," cautioned Tobias. "Not now. Anwir, what a timely meeting. Please join us."

"Hello. Ra, what brings you back so soon?"

"I'm only doing what you told me Karoon ordered…that my mission to Earth was complete and to return with what I learned."

"Why would I tell you something like that?"

"Anwir, I mean no disrespect, but you yourself have called me efficient." With an almost imperceptible contemptuous twitch of his eyebrow, Tobias kept his tone calm and collected. "I made a memorandum for the record after our last meeting; so it's easy enough to check. However, I do recall that we all agreed I was in charge of communication—just to cut down the confusion, you understand."

Before he could reply, the smug look on Anwir's face quickly turned to desperation at the site of the bald-headed deity making his way to the elevator. It was Karoon.

Karoon scanned the group and spied Ra. He struggled to keep his voice flat and emotionless, but the piercing glare in his blood-red orbs left nothing to the imagination.

"Must deities hold meetings in the lobby when there is ample space on the tenth floor?"

"No, sir," mumbled Anwir. "We were just about to move in that direction."

"Then I suggest you follow me into the elevator. I'm headed that way now."

When the elevator doors opened, Karoon was the first to exit. The small procession followed him down the hallway into his office suite. Taking care to keep the huge mosaic floor tile with the ostrich feather between them, he walked over and took a seat in the leather upholstered chair that was nestled within the well of his desk, then motioned Ra to sit in one of the mahogany wood leather wingback chairs that faced his desk.

"Ra, sit here. The rest of you take seats around the conference table."

Ra watched as Karoon leaned back in his chair, then studied the faces of the deities seated around the table. Finally he turned toward Ra and asked, "Who gave you permission to return?"

"Anwir, sir."

Karoon's gaze turned toward Anwir. When he spoke, the tone of his deep baritone voice became thick with anger.

"Anwir, who gave *you* permission?"

"Isfet."

The answer was met with silence. Karoon never changed his expression. He looked at Anwir and huffed, "When did you start taking orders from Isfet?"

Anwir crouched down in his chair with a look of sheer terror in his black orbs.

Karoon eyed Ra, sighed and said, "It's not your fault that you didn't complete your mission as I expected. Pity that your time in Jamaica was cut short. No matter. What did you learn while in the human body suit?"

Ra recalled that time in his office when he first met Karoon—his comment about the discovery of confidential information and the oath he made him swear. *Your own words will come back to haunt you,* he thought, as he watched Karoon with wry amusement and replied, "Sir, you have no reason to be concerned. With the measures you put in place, it's just a matter of time before the underground crumbles into history. Of course, with more time…but what's done is done. A different body suit would be needed if I were to go back. The experience for the human was draining, more so than we imagined. Another attempt would be fatal. But I assure you there's no need. George Patel is one of your most loyal children."

"Really?" Karoon studied the bright violet and lavender blue layers of Ra's energy field until he spotted telltale whiffs of muddy yellow-green, harbingers of deceit he was intimately familiar with. *Lying little sprite!* "Well…that's good. That's *very* good news. Nothing more to add?"

"No, sir."

"Well, Ra, you've earned your reward." Karoon's full lips curved into a broad smile that exposed the tips of his perfect white teeth. "It's just a matter of processing the paperwork, but I'm moving you to the next step. Starting tomorrow, you'll officially become my apprentice. Congratulations. You might as well get settled into your office space."

No sooner had the announcement been made when Ra felt a sharp pricking sensation on his right forearm near his elbow. He rolled up his sleeve to find a finished tattoo in the shape of an ostrich feather, hollow shaft pointing downward. The process had been performed so subtly that no one noticed. Except the deity seated next to him, who remained silent.

In the meantime, smiles and handshakes went all around, with the exception of Anwir, who somehow managed to leave the room without being noticed.

Ra motioned Tobias to follow him out into the hallway. Karoon had settled down in his office for an indefinite time, so it was a given that he would overhear anything said in the small work room. They walked in silence to the terrace lounge. It was still early, but the double doors were already open. When they walked in, they had the entire space to themselves.

Ra moved toward a corner table across the room, and Tobias followed. They pulled their chairs close together so both could face the door. Sitting within each others' energy fields, Tobias' violet eyes sparkled as he teased Ra.

"Well, *Lord* Ra, what did you make of George?"

Ra laughed softly. "He's…something special." His emerald green eyes twinkled with the memory of time spent with George. "I never believed I could appreciate the experience of a lesser dimensional being or—"

"Call him a friend?" Tobias prompted.

Ra shrugged and replied, "That's right. At his request, I revealed my true self to him."

"What was his reaction?"

"Very accepting."

Tobias smiled and asked, "And what about adventure and excitement. Was that waiting for you down there?"

"Yes. It was more than I dreamed it would be. We got along just fine. In fact, I was sorry to leave, at least so abruptly."

"Did you encounter any distractions while learning how to be in touch with your feelings and emotions? Oh, wait a minute." Tobias read vibes from different layers of Ra's energy field like open books, when something about one layer caught his attention. He made no audible comment, but his violet eyes narrowed and a shadow suddenly clouded his jovial expression. It was fleeting, just for a second or two. When he moved to another layer, his expression brightened and the sound of his baritone laughter, smooth as black velvet, floated across the room. "Ah, yes, I see it. A very *interesting* distraction that happened maybe once with a human female temptress…Vera?"

At the mention of her name, a blitz of electric red hues flashed through Ra's layers. He scratched his head and thought, *I'll bet Tobias knows everything that happened in that booth at Jolly's.*

"Yes, as a matter of fact, I do. *Especially* in that booth. *Lord* Ra…*really*!" This time the sound of Tobias' laughter was surprisingly fine and pure, almost like the tinkling sound of fresh snow fall. "Don't worry about it. That particular connection with her wasn't exactly what I had in mind. Actions have consequences, but we won't discuss that now. Let's just say the experience became part of your personal growth and development." An impish grin spread across Tobias' mouth into his violet eyes. He flashed Ra a little smile. "You've lost your innocence. But I think you're closer than ever to discovering your true calling."

A blush of red crept across Ra's bright violet and lavender blue layers. Embarrassed, he flashed a little smile and nodded.

"Now, give me an update on conditions in Jamaica."

"Things are worse than we thought. Feelings and emotions, the drive to maintain independence and resist control—those desires define the human experience as they once defined ours. George confided certain things with me. Leaders in the underground spread the alarm among untouched humans in their areas. They use personal shielding techniques, but even with our assistance, their efforts can't last much longer."

Tobias gave him a thoughtful look. "I agree. Here in Sun City, our days and nights are longer than on Earth. While you were away, we confirmed that the control station is right here, in the subbasement of this building."

Ra's mouth suddenly went dry. He swallowed, then continued, "Right here where I'll be working?"

"Yes. We also discovered that electrical energy is stored in capacitors in the warehouse located directly behind the Field Office. That's where it's converted into electromagnetic energy and sent to Earth as shockwaves."

Tobias grew silent. "If we could only find a way to get into that control station, we could shut down the whole operation." He eyed Ra, then turned his head slightly, shifted his gaze and fixed it on a spot somewhere across the room. When he turned back, he looked at Ra with eyes that had a prideful inner glow. "My complements, *Lord* Ra, for a job well done."

Ra was starting to feel more capable, confident, and self-assured by the second. He hoped the sudden shower of bright orange that dappled his energy field told Tobias how much the compliment meant to him.

But there was more to tell.

"There is something else."

"What's that?"

"It's as you said. George is the leader of the untouched in Jamaica. They operate from Jolly's. When George made his rounds there, he always found a reason to go down to the basement. The building is old as humans reckon time, and there are many corridors. Secret spaces, concealed rooms. It was always so dusty down there, and the lighting was poor.

The walls were made of bricks. I asked him what he hoped to find, and he said it was to make sure that something in the bricks called mineral wool was still in place, that it was a special type of insulation that contained lead particles. Wouldn't contact with that be dangerous for humans?"

"Not if they used appropriate protective clothing. Otherwise, yes, it could be deadly."

Ra drew in a breath. "George promised me he would wash his hands thoroughly, but—"

Before he could finish, Tobias piped, "Lead…*lead*? That's what's in those protective devices they wear. Not enough to harm them but small quantities, just enough to neutralize the EMP's. They must use that area in the basement as a storage and shielding area, a safe space in case an event happens for patrons who don't have protective devices with them. Wait a minute. Did you say mineral wool?"

"Yes, that's what he said. But I still don't get it."

"Humans who have been normalized have already been exposed to the radiation generated by the EMP's. But, mineral wool! That protects groups of humans who are still at risk. Humans are more suited to work with the dense, heavy atoms of solid lead. It's dangerous, however mineral wool room insulation only contains trace atoms of lead. Humans are safe around it, as long as precautions are taken. Being etheric beings, those atoms are light and won't hurt us. In fact, they would pass right through us. If that's how Karoon plans to do us in, it won't work. As far as we know, the deities he's experimented on have proven that light workers are immune to normalizing. At least in that way—" Tobias began to say something but instead paused and exclaimed, "Humans and deities…we need to work together."

Ra sighed and said, "That's exactly what I told George. The best thing we can do is find a way to get into that control room and shut everything down."

Chapter 41

As Ra considered what Tobias said, he suddenly caught sight of a figure, a female deity standing by the doorway, patiently observing their interaction.

Her presence registered with Tobias, who groaned and rolled his eyes at her, then faked a smile hoping she wouldn't notice.

But she did.

Even from a distance, Ra could tell she was most likely a third plane deity like DaValla and Julian, but there was something about her that reminded him of the females back on Earth at Jolly's.

Maybe it was the way she moved—no, glided—as she came closer and closer to them. Slowly. Deliberately. Shapely hips swinging. Her squared-shouldered sashay was quite different than Vera's relaxed stroll or the hurried, short steps Lynette took as she tried not to be noticed.

She stopped next to their table and flashed a humorless smile, then wiggled her nose and purred, "So now I'm the first one who has to speak to you before you tell me hello? Alright. *Hello* Tobias. How are you, Tobias? What's new, Tobias?"

Tobias sighed and muttered, "Oh…hello. Please join us."

She flashed a little smile that was as dry as a desert. "Thanks, I believe I will. Wait a minute. Let me get comfortable," then reached for a chair at a nearby table, pulled it over, and wedged it between them. As she lowered herself gracefully onto the seat, Ra watched the above-the-knee hemline of her dress rise just enough to show off legs that were toned, long, and slender. The glint of a gold necklace fastened securely around her neck caught his attention. It had her name spelled out in delicate script letters—Maat.

Ra wasn't sure when it happened, but he began to notice details about Maat, even more so than he did with Lynette or Vera.

As cold as her demeanor seemed to be, she was definitely attractive. Possibly the same age as himself. Around five feet tall give or take. Her oval-shaped face was framed by hair that, when worn loose, would probably fall at least to her waist. Now it was swept up into a curly brown pony tail, secured by a red ribbon. Each delicate earlobe sported a small gold hoop earring that flashed when it caught the light just right. The lighting in the room was no match for the red hues of her energy field that accentuated the glow of the gold undertones of her creamy, cinnamon brown skin. And, the color of her lipstick…how the bright red, almost scarlet shade dramatized her full lips and screamed, *imagine what it would be like to use me as a playground for your tongue.*

As improbable as it was, Ra recognized the warmth of a stirring in his groin. He had felt it before, but that was because George felt it. That was on Earth. Such things didn't, *couldn't,* happen in Sun City.

Or *could* they?

Things were moving too fast, and that made him uncomfortable. So when Tobias chimed in, it gave him an opportunity to regain his composure.

Tobias made no attempt to hide the blank expression on his face. "It's been awhile. All's well?"

Ra didn't know how it happened, but when Maat spoke again the sound of her voice was even more captivating and seductive.

"So-so. You know how it goes. Karoon sends his greetings."

With a flick of her wrist, she extended a perfectly manicured index finger painted red to complement her lipstick, pointed it at Ra, feigned ignorance and asked, "And who are you?"

Before he could answer, Tobias replied, "This is Ra, uh, *Lord* Ra. He has just completed his probationary period for the Creator God Apprentice job. Lord Ra, this is Maat, Karoon's, uh, Executive Secretary."

It startled Ra when, without warning, Maat scooted her chair in his direction. He hoped she hadn't noticed his lingering appraisal of the way her generous, creamy, cinnamon brown cleavage peaked out from beneath her plunging neckline.

"Nice to meet you, sir. I'm sure we'll be seeing a lot of each other."

For a second, Ra's eyebrows knitted together into a frown. He averted his eyes, then casually glanced back in her direction, smiled, and in a baritone voice that was more silvery than usual, said "Why so formal. Just call me Ra."

Chapter 42

Tobias knew Maat would park her essence on that chair until she got what she came for. He turned to Ra and said, "My apologies. I have an appointment elsewhere, but Ra, there's something I need to discuss with you before I go." He shot Maat a sideways glance and said, "You won't mind, will you?"

"Not in the least." She caressed Ra with her gaze and murmured, "I'll wait right here until you return."

Tobias led the way into the hallway away from Maat's prying stare. Finding a secluded corner where they wouldn't be disturbed, he cautioned, "Don't trust her. She's Karoon's mistress. I don't like to spread gossip, but there's something you need to know about her."

An unexpected sound in the hallway caused him to pause and slightly raise his eyebrows, then lower them when he realized it was only the building settling. "The walls here are thin. Sound passes easily from one room to another. What I'm going to tell you is secondhand information, but I believe it's reliable. They say Maat charmed her way into Karoon's office, unannounced, stood in front of his desk, looked at him and declared in that low raspy voice of hers, 'Let's get it on, big daddy.' Feelings of insecurity hidden behind an aggressive come-on. She was from the same dark corner of the NoWhere as his minions. That's why he sensed a familiar vibe about her that was also her weakness—her ego. It was almost as large as his, and that discovery let him know how to exploit her charms for his advantage. He fed that ego, offered her power and recognition as his trophy mistress. You see, he wasn't satisfied with what he had already accomplished. He wanted more, and Maat could help him fulfill that desire."

His voice took on a guarded tone. "It's no secret that she oversees all the catchers in Sun City, the ones who spy on us and report back to Karoon. I know because I've overheard them talking in his office, of course without their knowledge. We keep her at a discreet distance because like Anwir, we can't trust her."

Tobias waited to see Ra's reaction. When his expression didn't change, he continued. "I suppose you're thinking there are two sides to every story. And you'd be right. To hear her tell it, she was the one who cast a spell over him, pulled him into her dark red energy field, made him eat out of her hands before he knew what hit him. Karoon was just a means to an end. What she really longed for was something no deity she knew had ever experienced. Something more than the mental thrill of erotic gratification. She was obsessed with finding a way to make her erotic fantasies real. You see, she was a nobody who longed to be remembered as somebody. Karoon bored her, but she would endure until a better vehicle came along." Tobias paused, his violet eyes reflective. "I hope you see where I'm going with this. She's got a thirst for instant knowledge and pleasure, a perfect storm that may well lead to her downfall. Her words drip with poison honey. She's a seductress. That's her true calling. She sees nothing wrong with it. And Ra, you are definitely next on her list."

With that, Tobias made a hasty exit down the hallway leaving Ra on his own with a female deity—the very definition of temptation.

Chapter 43

Ra made his way back to the double doors of the terrace lounge. He stood in the doorway aware that other deities, mostly dark workers, had come in during his absence, but searching for one in particular…Maat. Was it his growing confidence that caused him to ignore Tobias' warning? He remained motionless for a long second, then made his way to the table and sat down beside her.

A familiar voice, one he hadn't heard in a long time, called to him in his mind. *My old nemesis, desire, reaches out to tempt me,* he groaned. The low, deep, raspy voice was back.

You know you want it. She's a dark worker, but don't let that stop you. Show her what you learned in Jamaica. Who knows? It might even be fun.

"I heard you were actually on Earth in a human body suit? And in Jamaica!"

Ra stared at Maat in disbelief. and thought, *Did she eavesdrop on the prompt given by the voice in my mind?*

"Yes, it was enlightening."

"I can't imagine going anywhere near that place." Maat gave him a sideways glance and asked, "The human perspective. What was it like? Tell me, is it true that humans actually make thoughts real?"

"I'm not sure what you mean."

Maat leaned closer to him and casually crossed her legs, then relaxed one on top of the other to highlight her shapely calf muscle and said, "Are they in touch with their own and others feelings and emotions, or do they just go through the motions?"

Suddenly Ra felt an urge to rub the back of his neck. He did and was surprised to find his fingers moist with clammy sweat. What began as a conversation was starting to feel more like an interrogation, and he was anxious for it to end.

"Uh, they are."

"So you can really communicate with humans through portals?"

"Yes, as we do with other deities."

"Does that let you experience things as they do?"

"Yes."

"Was your human intimate with another human while you were in him?"

"Why do you ask?"

"Oh, just curious. It's getting crowded in here. Why don't we go back to your office, and you can fill me in with all the details."

Chapter 44

Maat sensed she had some kind of chemistry with Ra. But he seemed so reserved, so different from either Karoon or herself. She didn't know much about Ra, only what Karoon sent through the portal when he and Tobias were in the hallway. *The reception in there is lousy. Karoon's voice sounded so different, like he had sandpaper in the back of his throat…almost like a croak. But I do recall him saying to find out if Ra was holding something back. What was the word he used? Interrogate him.*

She'd have to use intuition and cunning to figure-him out. *This time I won't ignore that sinking feeling in the pit of my stomach that happens when I'm about to mess up. I've got to slow down and consider every possible angle as I write a mental script for him that will get me what I want. I write scripts for everyone. It's entertaining. The one I wrote for myself kept me focused on what I had to do to claw and scheme my way from the NoWhere to this place…from being a nobody to a somebody with all the trappings that go with it. I'll get Ra to teach me—that is if he really knows the secret—how to be in touch with his own and others' feelings and emotions. Aside from him, that will take me where no other dark or light worker has ever gone. With what I learn from him, I can write my own ticket, come out from inside the fortress I built that hides my true self. I'll teach others, but for a price. I'll be the one in control. There's much more to me than meets the eye. They'll worship me for the superior being that I am, and who knows…I might even replace Karoon as their goddess. Goddess Maat. The sound has a nice ring to it.*

They walked in silence down the hallway and back to what had become Ra's office space. The door leading into Karoon's office suite was closed. He had already left for the day, but not before he cluttered Ra's desk with a variety of folders for him to work on.

Maat walked right in and took a seat at the small conference table. Karoon's agenda quickly faded from her memory to be replaced by one of her own. *I don't care what Karoon wants. Ra is mine to enjoy as I please. Consequences…,yes, but only if discovered.*

She watched Ra from behind as he worked, especially the V-shaped taper of muscles that extended downward from his broad shoulders to end in a trim waist. *He's got a lean, fit, muscular physique beneath his form-fitted clothing. That's the kind of erotic strength and energy that fuels my fantasies. I wonder what it would be like to rub my body against his creamy, golden brown, luminous skin, touched by a glint of lavender blue, slightly lighter than the rich layers of bright violet hues that comprise his energy field?*

The door leading from the hallway creaked. Ra turned around just in time to realize that Maat had walked back to the door and pushed it closed. He watched as she walked to the conference table and leaned against it. "I sense there's more to your human adventure than you're willing to say. But I know how to keep a secret. It doesn't matter to me what side you're on. There's no one in here except you and me, and I won't tell. They say you're a rebel. That *excites* me. I'm tired of living a life that's beneath me," she sighed. "Teach me how to bridge the divide. Make it *real*… for me."

"Are you sure that's what you want, because there's no turning back."

"Yes, and I hope it won't take all day. I have other things to do."

Ra smiled and thought, *This will be the first lesson of many more to come.* "Then let's begin."

He reached into her mind and opened a portal between them.

Chapter 45

Ra's gaze swept up and down Maat's curvaceous figure. Classic. Sultry. Wrapped in a black gossamer dress. He walked over until he stood next to her. Their eyes met. *Your eyes…dark brown, almond-shaped, rimmed in black eyeliner, smoldering, deep. Mesmerizing. They pull me toward you like a moth to a flame. It makes me dizzy.* He reached out thinking it was the table he grabbed when it was her, pulling him down on top of her into a more relaxed position.

Ra remembered how it was back on Earth when he was inside George that night at Jolly's. The scene replayed in his mind like a movie on a screen. This time it wasn't just a movie. He wasn't just a bystander who capitalized on something someone else started, someone else's vibes. The vibes were his. They felt just like those that shot up and down his spine when he was inside George. *It doesn't matter that we're within feet of the office of the tyrant himself. I'm ready to teach. But is it right that a dark worker should be my first student?*

There was a time when he would have thrown caution to the wind. Now he hesitated, found himself weighing the pros and cons of accepting Maat's sensual invitation. Performance under pressure was something he wasn't looking forward to. From somewhere deep inside his essence came cautious advice. A baritone voice as smooth as black velvet whispered, *Experience is the best teacher. Be a vessel for that information. Bring it back to us. You'll know what to do with it when the time is right.* It never occurred to him that *us* might also include dark workers.

"Maat, this is what you wanted. Well, I won't disappoint you." He opened a portal between them and said, "Relax. We'll take it one step at a time. Just do what I tell you. Stroke my back with your hands."

Maat did as directed. Ra felt her hands glide across the fabric of his shirt, across the outline of his broad shoulders, and down his back valley to his waist as he pulled back slightly, then rolled under her on the table. His baritone voice was deep, resonant, incredibly gorgeous as he murmured, "Now, get on top of me. Relax. Let go. Try to act on your thoughts, and let's see what happens."

As she straddled him, his hands wandered under her dress. His fingers rubbed up her thighs to find her moist place, then lightly massaged up and down, side to side.

Without being told to do so, Ra felt Maat reach down and unbutton his shirt, already moist with sweat, then comb her fingers through his jet-black chest hair...play with his coils and beard shaped into a perfect curve at his cheeks and square jawline. When he gazed into her eyes, he saw that a vacant expression had replaced the mystery that once mesmerized him. Ignoring the change and wanting to believe they were making progress, he smiled then shifted his weight and guided her fingers to his zipper. "Unzip my pants."

She did, and slipped her fingers inside to feel his cock. It was already turgid between his legs. She started to pull her hands away when he gently took them in his, pressed them to his groin, and wondered, *Why is she fighting me?* He looked at her and murmured, "What does it do to your body when you touch me here?"

He began to read her vibes and frowned. *She's hiding something from me. Instead of relaxing and letting go, she's actually looking through those windows and admiring the skyline of the City! Going through the motions. Is that all this means to you? Is that all I mean to you?*

"Not quite there yet?" Ra's eyes displayed a look of bewildered disappointment. "Well, let's move on to the next step. Take off your dress."

His directive broke Maat out of her momentary reverie. She slipped her dress over her head and let it drop to the floor. The red glow of her nude, ethereal body shimmered in the subdued light that filtered in through the windows. As Ra caressed her creamy, cinnamon brown skin, he caught whiffs of heady, feminine musk scent mixed with spicy cinnamon-scented perfume. He reached up and cupped her naked breasts in his hands, moved his fingers round and round to trace the outlines of each dusky areola, then gently ran the tip of his tongue in circles around each nipple as he nibbled, sucked, and massaged until they became sensitive and swollen. Only then did her expression relax.

The vacant look in her eyes began to disappear as she sighed and moaned. "It feels like waves of intense energy are rushing through my essence. My heart is racing faster than in my wildest fantasies."

Now, that's more like it, thought Ra. A look of satisfaction twinkled in his emerald green eyes. He put his arms around her and murmured, "Bend down toward me so I can kiss you." He pulled her close to him as the tip of his tongue parted her red lips then slipped inside her mouth to explore between moist breaths that were slow and deep. His arousal pulsed against her bare bottom, and she didn't protest when he quickly slid his hands down around her hips, pulled them toward his soft full lips, and slipped his tongue between the folds in her pubic area.

"Press down. Let your body rub against my tongue."

She did, and Ra felt the pull of her pubic hair as it rubbed against his beard. Maat began to rock back and forth, which sent electric chills and warm tingles from his head to his toes. When she slid her body down, reached back, and began to stroke his growing need with her hands, he rolled on top of her to let her guide him inside. Her muscles released and tensed, and her back arched upward to receive him as he exploded into her, again and again.

"What are you doing to me?"

The glow of Ra's emerald green eyes returned her gaze through partially closed lids. "I'm not doing anything to you. *You're* making it happen. Sensations baby. Connections between thoughts, feelings and emotions."

But too many and all at once. Panicked, Maat muttered, "This is a nightmare. I don't understand…"

Ra knew Maat needed to calm down. Her thoughts were now real feelings and emotions, and she needed to talk about what that meant, give it a name and control the flow so it wouldn't overwhelm her.

"Talk to me. Tell me what you feel and…"

"I—"

The lesson came to an abrupt halt with the echo of footsteps coming down the hallway.

"Ra, I thought you might be interested in—" The sound of Anwir's low, deep, raspy voice trailed off to an incoherent squeak as he barged into Ra's office space unannounced. "Uh…I just thought…but…well…I'll…oh…be back later."

A blinding clash of passionate red against dazzling bright violet and lavender. The flurry of limbs entwined within limbs. Embarrassed expressions. Rumpled clothes scattered about the floor. The spectacle happening on the conference table was too much for him to process. Anwir froze, took a step backward into the hallway, and kept on going.

Maat retrieved her dress, then turned to Ra and said, "Thanks. I'm sure I can take it from here."

"No, Maat, you've only begun. There's more to—"

Listening but not slowing her pace, she quickly dressed and headed toward the door, then turned and winked at Ra. "Maybe I'll see you later? If not, well, it's been fun. I'm sure this will get back to Karoon. Don't worry about it. I'll handle him. You just go on with your duties."

Chapter 46

Karoon's blood-red orbs narrowed almost to slits and shot fire with a look that would melt the strongest metal. *So, Maat, the mental thrill of erotic gratification I shared with you wasn't good enough.* When he spoke to Anwir, his deep, baritone voice had all the composure of a seething volcano.

"Who have you told this to besides me?"

"No one, sir, but they were rather loud. Others might wonder."

"We'll just keep this between us for now. Understand? And, Anwir, your discretion won't go unrewarded."

"Thank you, sir." *My days of being an afterthought in your eyes are over.* "As you wish."

In an instant, Karoon knew what he had to do. His growing lust for revenge fueled dark intentions against Maat. *Ra's just my apprentice, a sprite, innocent about such matters. But Maat. I know this is your fault. How could you do this to me? After all I've done for you.* His full lips quivered as he struggled to remain stoic. *What's the worst thing I could do to hurt you? Send you packing back to that dark corner of the NoWhere you called home? No. Better to take away all you worked for. Your status, bid for power, delusion that good looks and enchanting ways mean more to me than absolute loyalty. I'll make you the laughing stock of the entire Court, if not Sun City. There are other female deities who would consider it an honor to be paraded around on my arm. I'll choose the pick of the litter and do for her what I did for you. My next mistress will appreciate the wisdom of loyalty and choose a wiser path.*

True to his word, it didn't take long for him to bring Lynette on board at The Court as his personal Administrative Assistant. One day, he summoned her to his office.

"Lynette, would you please come in here."

"Yes, sir."

She stood up, grabbed her notepad and pencil, and headed toward his door. Her steps, once hurried and short, were now confident, almost a strut. Just as she was about to cross the threshold, she paused mid-stride.

"Sir?"

Gone were his translucent glowing layers of gold. His true murky brown, muddy yellow-green energy field greeted her as he leaned back in his leather-upholstered chair, partially nestled into the well of his executive desk.

He watched Lynette as she entered his office suite. His lips curved into a broad smile as he turned on the charisma and crooned, "Please, come in and close the door. I know it's short notice, but something's come up. I'll need you to work tomorrow, well into the evening. Maybe very late. Of course, I'll make arrangements for dinner here in the office."

"No problem, sir."

Karoon casually pointed to one of the leather wingback chairs that faced his desk. "Have a seat."

Ever since their first meeting at the Field Office, he planned to keep Lynette close to him. It was true that he wanted to find out what she overheard that day in the hallway. Her purity and wide-eyed innocence was always a turn-on for the predator in him. Of course, he never did anything about it.

Until now.

After a few seconds he rose, walked around and sat on one edge of his desk with his legs crossed, ankle over knee just inches from Lynette. Pausing for a second, he flashed his signature smile and declared, "I want you to be my Executive Secretary."

Her hazel eyes grew large as she looked at him and stammered, "But…that's Maat's position."

"It was. She's been reassigned." Karoon glanced down at his well-manicured nails. "I need someone with a stronger sense of loyalty. Do you have a strong sense of loyalty?"

"I'm not quite sure what you mean, sir, but I'm so grateful for all you've done for me. This promotion was like a new start in life. I've tried my best to follow all your directives and—"

Before she could finish, he reached out, touched her lightly on one shoulder, then grabbed her and pulled her up close to him, which sent patches of pale yellow surging throughout the luminous hues of her own layers. "Well, here's a *new* directive for you to follow."

Lynette grimaced at the cold feel of his long, slender fingers and backed away. Karoon moved toward her again but suddenly paused at the sound of a sharp gasp and a muttered curse.

Maat stood in the doorway. Observant. Livid. Silent as Lynette turned and without comment, brushed past her and into the outer office.

Chapter 47

Angry. Confused. Humiliated. Maat stormed into Karoon's office.

"Karoon!"

"Shut up, you slut! I heard what happened in that room between you and my apprentice."

Perhaps an attitude of indifference will soften his heart. Maat batted her long, black eyelashes and scoffed, "He means nothing to me."

"He probably doesn't. That's not the point."

"I did what you told me to do. You told me to find out if he was holding something back from you."

Karoon eyed her, his face hardened and his blood-red eyes icy cold. "I told you to *interrogate* him…not *fuck* him."

"But I thought…the voice in my mind. I thought it was your voice."

"What voice?"

"So loud, but no, it wasn't you. It was almost a croak, like the speaker had sandpaper in the back of his throat."

"Isfet!"

"Even so," she scoffed, "who are you to criticize me? I was the one who made you look good, but now you're coming on to what's her name—Lynette, that little thing from the steno pool." The name of her presumed rival came out in a hiss. "It won't be long before you find a reason to arrange one of your late-night work sessions with her. How well I know what happens at those sessions!"

Karoon bristled when Maat became unapologetic. He stared at her, his full lips formed into a voiceless laugh.

"As a matter of fact, I've got one scheduled tomorrow night. Maat, you forget who I am. Now that you mention her name…Lynette. Lovely, isn't she? So sweet with her yellow, baby blue, and white bubbles. And her eyes. Hazel, large as saucers. Did you know her eyes have flecks of gold at the center? A little golden comb holds her hair in place. I'll have to remember to get a new one for her. She will assume your position starting today. And if you're not careful, you'll find yourself cleaning toilets and scrubbing floors."

"I'll have my revenge, Karoon. I'll have my *revenge!*"

"Don't do anything stupid. There's no corner of the Realm where you can hide. I'll always find you and make you wish…well, you'll *never* have peace-of- mind."

Maat turned and stomped out into the hallway. *News of my demotion will fly around here like a blast of solar wind. Karoon, you've gone too far. If I'm going down, I'll take you with me. After all, I know secrets and just who to tell them to!*

Chapter 48

Tobias, meet me in the terrace lounge. Important!

The urgent tone in the note Maat slipped him as they passed in the hallway made Tobias wonder, *What's she up to now?*

As he walked into the lounge, he saw her sitting alone at the same table he and Ra were seated at the first time she met him.

"Maat, what can I do for you?" His greeting was polite but short.

"Sit, please. I guess you heard what Karoon did to me."

"Gossip is not my thing, but I understand rumors are being passed."

"Well, I know that you have no reason to trust me, but I've had a change of heart."

Heart? Maat? You're right. There is no reason I should trust you. However, I'm curious, so I'll hear what you have to say.

"Please go on."

"There's something I need to know. You're a light worker…a Singularity?"

"That's correct."

"I've watched you. Some call you a visionary, say that you come from a place of pure positive energy. That you have the rarest of vibes…gold, tinged with white and purple. A deity with a gentle demeanor who is far from weak. How can you support Karoon's agenda?"

"Do you really expect me to answer that?"

"No, not really. You, more than most, understand things are not always as they seem. I don't blame you for not believing anything I say. But this you can believe. If your cause is different than Karoon's, then I can help you do what must be done."

"Revenge, Maat? Is that what you're after?"

"That's part of it. But truthfully, I've always thought that as a leader, Sun City could do a lot better."

"What do you propose?"

"Let me tell you what I know. Karoon is a jealous and envious tyrant. He will destroy anything he can't control, or better yet, use for his own benefit. He's looking for a way to control light workers here in Sun City. His minions already control most humans through a process called normalizing. A few retain their independence, but not for long. Mind you, I'm not accusing you of anything. But if you're interested, the heart of the operation is right here in this building."

"I know that." Tobias' response was short and dry.

"Well, this is something you might now know. Go down the blocked-off corridor off the first-floor lobby, the one marked Authorized Personnel Only. It will take you to the subbasement and the control room. That's where all the action happens. What can shut the whole thing down is in that room. Look for a large console that has one monitor and only two buttons. When you see it, you'll know what to do. The capacitors that hold the electrical energy that's converted into electromagnetic energy are in the warehouse behind the Field Office. They will be automatically disabled when you shut the console down."

Well, I'll be…How did I miss knowing you, a dark worker and catcher, could be sympathetic to our cause? Thoroughly attentive, Tobias asked, "What about the satellite?"

"Don't worry. You'll disable it as well. It will burn up as it reenters Earth's atmosphere. There's only one door to the control room. They keep it locked. But for the right price, I can get you the *key to the kingdom*."

"And the right price would be?"

"To see Karoon stripped of his authority and banished with his minions to that dark corner of the NoWhere they came from."

"*All* of his minions?"

"Yes, every…last…one."

"Would there be no room for mercy?"

"None."

"And, peace-of-mind? Would revenge bring that to you?"

"Yes, it most certainly would."

Tobias took a deep breath, released it and said, "I believe we can do business together. When can you deliver the key?"

"A late-night work session has been scheduled for tomorrow. I'll make up some excuse to be around his office before it starts, maybe that I'm collecting my things. I know where he keeps that key. Then I'll go out into the hallway and stand where I can watch Lynette at her desk. As soon as she goes into his office, I'll get the key, come down to the lobby, and drop it behind that tall potted plant. Watch for me."

Chapter 49

The next morning at Tobias' urging, a hastily planned meeting convened in the terrace lounge on the tenth floor. The place was slowly filling up with dark workers, which made it hard to understand DaValla's deep baritone voice, lowered almost to a whisper.

"Can Maat be trusted?"

"My sentiments exactly," piped Julian. He sat beside DaValla, his hazel eyes wide as he scanned the area for those who might want to listen to their conversation.

Tobias hesitated for a second, then said, "If it will help our cause, I say let's take advantage of her newfound change of heart and give her offer a chance."

DaValla's silver-gray eyes were almost closed in silent reflection. "Things done out of revenge are often self-serving. What does she want in return?"

"Only that Karoon be stripped of his authority and banished with his minions to that dark corner of the NoWhere they came from. She's going to get the key tonight before Karoon starts his work session with Lynette."

Tobias studied the faces of his comrades. "I'm to be in the lobby on the first floor, watching for her. So be in the area and look for me. She'll make the delivery and drop the key behind that tall potted plant. When that happens, we'll make our move." He looked at Julian and DaValla and said, "I suspect Karoon and his dark workers to retaliate. Pass the word among as many light workers as possible to alert leaders within the untouched community on Earth. Their assistance will be needed to help humans cope with the change in their behavior that will happen when those shockwaves stop coming and the effects wear off."

His gaze swept across the faces of his comrades knowing the price each might pay in case of failure, then added, "Tonight. Be ready to position yourselves near that blocked-off corridor, the one marked Authorized Personnel Only. According to Maat, it leads to the subbasement. That's where the control station is."

DaValla and Julian looked at each other, then turned their gaze toward Tobias. He had never led them wrong in the past. There was no reason to suspect he would start now.

Tobias eyed Ra thoughtfully. "You've got a stake in this. What do you have to say?"

"I say we do what we must to get that key and shut that madness down."

True to her word, when Maat walked through the lobby, she dropped a key behind the tall potted plant, then made a hasty exit from the building.

From where he stood near the reception desk, Tobias watched her, then casually strolled over, retrieved the key, and put it in his pants pocket.

No dark worker suspected that a light worker would dare plot to break into a restricted area. After all, in their minds light workers were disenfranchised, powerless, fearful, and easily intimidated.

That night, four light workers would prove them wrong.

With the colors and hues of their energy fields toned down until they were almost transparent, Tobias and the others made their way to the end of the corridor, then down two flights to the subbasement. As luck would have it, a shift change was already in progress. Absent-minded as usual, the few dark workers milling around didn't notice them as they stood before the plain wooden door. It was locked, but when Tobias slipped the key into the keyhole, it opened without difficulty.

Bleeps. Clicks. Whines. Hums. The large room vibrated with a life of its own.

Tobias whispered, "Spread out. Find that command console."

An array of lights, some blinking, some fixed, peeked through cold, impersonal ambience enough to reveal a network of small consoles arranged in a circle formation around one large console. Each of the smaller consoles had multiple monitors that showed graphical displays of delivery schedules and the status of the satellite and capacitors being charged. But the large console in the middle of the circle was their target. It had one monitor with two buttons that relayed one of two administrative commands to the main system: power on or system shut down.

That command console was their target.

With Tobias in the lead and Ra close on his heels, they sprinted toward the target. Tobias was the first to arrive. Just a second away from touching the system shut down button, he paused, turned toward Ra, nodded and declared, "Sprite, it's time that you know who I am."

For what seemed an eternity but was in reality only a long second, all activity in the room slowed to a grinding halt. Dark workers froze in mid-motion. Lights stopped flashing. All sound ceased.

For the first time, Tobias revealed his true self to Ra…the power and glory that was his alone to rightfully claim.

Engulfed in a whirling fiery golden maelstrom of amber and pure white, ribbons of purple, regal and majestic, swirled around a form much larger than the one Ra had come to know as Tobias. His hair was still white but more like wool, and his eyes sparkled with the deep purple of semi-precious gemstones. Standing there in all his magnificence and glory, he smiled and said, "Remember, service to others over self-interest. You are my son, in whom I am well pleased. I declare that this is your moment. I've given you my favor…now, step into your power and own it. Push the button."

Ra was awed. As the revelation of Tobias' true identity seared into his mind, he obediently pushed the system shut down button and locked it into place.

The dark workers quickly snapped out of their stupor. But it was too late. As predicted, chaos erupted. A frenzied display of shouts and movement. Perfect cover for Tobias and his small group to make a speedy and smooth departure.

Chapter 50

During the days that followed, the blame game went into high gear. Karoon, of course, was livid. *It's all fallen apart. Dark workers and catchers…absent-minded, useless creatures.*

No dark worker or catcher wanted to be held accountable for the fiasco that caused his master plan to come to a grinding halt. Even those who assisted in the downfall packed and left Sun City to take up residence elsewhere.

Karoon retreated to the huge office space that had become part of his identity. He cringed whenever a sound came from the hallway. It reminded him that it was just a matter of time before the light workers would come to get him. Without the threat of his ultimate method of control or his minions, he had no leverage with which to intimidate or incite fear.

And, he was right.

Early one morning, he stood before the wall of floor-to-ceiling windows and looked out at the unparalleled view of the Karoonsville skyline bathed in its usual dismal splendor. Then he turned around and surveyed the expensive office furnishings; the huge executive desk and leather-upholstered chair, the marble floor, the huge mosaic tile with the perfectly symmetrical ostrich feather, brownish gray in color, hollow shaft pointing downward emblazoned on it.

One lone deity had been standing in the doorway for quite some time, silently observing the fallen tyrant. Encased in gold, tinged with white and purple hues of energy, he was radiant, commanding…formidable. Casually dressed in a black suit and jacket, tufts of curly black chest hair peeked out from beneath the top two buttons on his white shirt, unbuttoned far enough to reveal the outline of a well-defined pectoral muscle. His posture, stance, everything about him screamed, *It's not a matter of your vibe or mine. My vibe is all that counts.*

He eyed Karoon. The pity in his violet eyes was the only thing that betrayed his stoic facial expression as he said in a baritone voice as smooth as black velvet, "It's time for you to go."

Karoon returned his stare and thought, *I always suspected you were not who you professed to be…that you were much higher than a third plane deity. Even higher than myself.*

"First plane, to be precise." Tobias' voice was unwavering.

"Then that would mean you are…" Karoon's voice trailed off mid-sentence. He blinked and in a tone that was measured and unemotional muttered, "At last, we meet, my Lord, my father. So, this is how it ends for me?"

The one he had come to know as Tobias answered. "Choices do have eternal repercussions."

Caught off-guard, Karoon struggled to retain his composure. "I was never to be good enough in your eyes…never to be worthy."

"On the contrary. As sprites, both you and Ra were the youngest in your second plane colonies. My love for you was no less than for him. My wish no less noble or positive.

"Service to others over self-interest…*my* vibe, not yours. Listen to *my* voice. Choose an *honorable* path. That's all it took for you to receive the blessing. But, I couldn't give it to you. You stepped into your power and claimed it, but chose to go in a destructive direction. You became one of my fallen children, but I still hoped you would realize the error of your ways and repent. But no. You left your homeland, ventured beyond the seventh plane into a dark corner of the NoWhere and found your brother, Isfet. Well, you were both second plane deities gone astray. I gave you free will, favored you with gifts of gab and charisma, and what did you do? Misused them. Abused them. Together you deceived a group of marginalized misfits, manipulated them, convinced them to sell the most precious things they possessed—emotions and feelings—for the price of your dreams of conquest. Both of you fed on their worship and praise. Both of you became purveyors of destruction and injustice—your true callings. Anger, jealousy, hate, and chaos became your vibes.

"It pained me to see the beautiful emerald green eyes I gave both you and Isfet gradually transform into blood-red orbs. I could only wait, watch, hope you would change and be worthy of the deities I suspected you were capable of being. Until this very moment, I believed. But neither of you asked for forgiveness. That told me you armor was still incomplete. Like blades of swords being forged, your character still needed a bit of…tempering."

Karoon lowered his gaze, then raised it to meet *The Almighty's* violet stare. "And, Maat. What of her?"

"A work in progress. She left with the others."

With Tobias in the lead, followed by Karoon, Ra, DaValla, and Julian, a procession of light workers flowed from The Court down the long winding street that stretched all the way to Aaru, the place where the sun rose. A mist with a fetid odor and clammy feel greeted them as they entered the open space. Muddy yellow and forest green with splashes of dull gray, it descended around Karoon. When he turned, his blood-red orbs swept over the crowd with unrepentant defiance. The shadow of a cruel grin passed across his cunning facial features. His full lips exposed the tips of perfect white teeth. Then, without a word or gesture, he stepped into the mist and as it became more translucent…simply disappeared.

Chapter 51

The crowd thinned as the day wore on. Those who remained at Aaru, the place where the sun rose, rejoiced as the fetid odor of the muddy yellow and forest green mist gradually faded. The sky over the entire City was already returning to its original vibrant pink and turquoise blue, and all sections of the street were once again paved in gold and in perfect condition.

The exquisite coolness of clean air pleased the light workers. Singularities and soulmates. They huddled together in small groups, and contemplated their individual and collective futures as citizens of *New* Sun City.

Everyone agreed that Tobias should lead them. As he considered their request, his violet eyes swelled with affection. They were his children, each and every one. Then an easy smile passed across his lips. He raised his hands to quiet the crowd, drew in a breath, exhaled, and began to speak.

"The voice of Karoon, the one who made false claims and offered empty promises, has been stilled. The discord and confusion he caused has come to an end. Let the healing process begin.

"You've got a long journey ahead of you to awaken what has been suppressed for too long. It won't be easy to repair the damage done by the false image of you Karoon created. But, through it all, I know you never lost your true selves. So that's a starting point.

"One day you will remember how to be in touch with your own and others feelings and emotions, how to make the connection to make thoughts real, how to use them to make wise decisions. They are the most precious gifts you possess…the very things that define you. Do that and once again be surrounded by beauty and goodness. But you must learn how to bridge the divide and temper the full intensity of sensation. Be of good cheer. There is one among you who already knows the secret."

He nodded in Ra's direction, then directed his attention back to the crowd. "Ra is the vessel for that information. He learned it in the most unlikely place possible…among humans on a planet in the fourth plane called Earth. Deities and humans. Together you worked to defeat Karoon. Deities and humans. Both free at last.

"What Ra did took courage, discipline, discernment…and *faith*. Service to others over self…that is his true calling and also his destiny. One day he will be celebrated as the one who worked to create something greater than himself." He turned to face Ra and said, "Teach them, trigger in them what has for so long been dormant."

Epilogue

Sighs of relief could be heard coming from Julian and DaValla as they followed Ra and the deity they knew as Tobias. Their heads bobbed up and down as they reviewed the events of the day.

No one except Ra knew Tobias' true identity. Tobias and *The Almighty.* They were the same. As they walked back to The Court, Tobias turned to Ra and quietly murmured, "I'll be absent, at least for a while. There's unfinished business to attend in the NoWhere. You see, I haven't given up on Karoon. Then there's the matter of Anwir and Isfet and…"

"Maat?"

"Yes, Maat. I know how you feel about her, regardless of the cost and, well, I'm always willing to forgive. By the way, look at your right arm."

Ra plucked at the cuffs of his shirt sleeves. The tiny tattoo in the shape of an ostrich feather, hollow shaft pointing downward, had vanished.

Tobias grinned and said, "You're *my* apprentice now. We'll rebuild Sun City as I created it to be. By the way, my journey will take me near the colonies of your home plane. I'll spend some time with Lias. I made a bet with him about something." His smooth baritone chuckle was just loud enough to be heard by Ra. "I'm sure he will be pleased."

"You know Lias?"

"Yes, he has been my faithful steward for quite some time."

"I don't think he'll be pleased that I missed the ritual."

"On the contrary. You see, Lias and I have a certain understanding. I insisted that he send you to Sun City before the ritual. Karoon and his minions…their vibes were only distractions. Many voices called to you, but mine was the one you chose to hear. Being able to discern which voice to follow was a test of your faith in me. It proved your loyalty to me. Lias didn't think you were ready to receive the blessing. But I knew you even before you tumbled from my eyes to find refuge in his outstretched arms. I knew all along that you wouldn't let distractions keep you from discovering your one true calling…that it was also your destiny and that you would choose to step into and claim the power I had already given you and do right by it. The ritual is only a formality. I'm well pleased with your performance. You have achieved full status as a second plane deity. Take your rightful place among the League of Stewards. Congratulations, *Lord Ra*."

Tobias turned and regarded Julian and DaValla, then added, "Remember, I'm never far away. Besides, you have them in your corner and light workers always stick together."

"And Earth, my Lord. What's going to happen to George and the underground?"

Tobias breathed a heavy sigh. "Your meeting with George was not by accident. I've had a relationship with his ancestors for generations. The way he was reared, the humble circumstances of his early life, the lessons he learned and advice he passed on to you…all so that he could be the conduit through which you received the secret you needed to learn to fulfill your destiny. You see, I always have a back-up plan. The road he and the others have chosen will be a difficult one to walk. However, they won't walk it alone. And who knows. Your path may cross his…again"

"My Lord, my father, you once told me that what you predict about the future always comes true." An infectious smile spread across Ra's lips and found its way into his emerald green eyes. "Can I look forward to that happening?"

The reassuring have-faith smile that floated across Tobias lips more than answered Ra's question.

"One day I hope to restore Aaru to its former glory. In the meantime, I suggest you operate from the office suite Karoon used at The Court. Now as to the furnishings. Any objection to making that high-backed chair in the Field Office a part of the permanent furnishings? You know, the one made of oak, heavily carved with elaborate ribbons and floral designs on scrolled arms and long cabriole legs, with the small, luxurious velvet pillow resting on top of the cane seat. I've grown rather fond of it. And I have another favor to ask."

"I'm listening."

Tobias, now known to Ra as *The Almighty*, smiled and said, "While I'm away, try not to succumb to any more temptations."

"Your *vibe*…now *mine!*"

The sound of *The Almighty's* smooth baritone chuckle was like music to Ra's ears. They walked, side by side, down the road paved in gold. In the distance the facade of The Court sparkled with crystal clarity. Every inch shimmered in light that appeared to be illuminated from somewhere within the building. Deep blue sapphire, fiery jasper, yellow agate, green emerald, black onyx, translucent red carnelian, greenish yellow chrysolite, pink beryl, amber topaz, orange jacinth, and red-rimmed amethyst.

It was as splendid as the first time Ra saw it.

As they got closer to the entrance, his attention was drawn to a figure that stood by the double doors.

It was female.

About the Author

Dr. Adah F. Kennon is a published author who is now from Las Vegas. Originally from Houston, Texas, she has also lived and worked in California and Maryland. Formally trained as a psychologist, professional mental health counselor, and voice-over actor, she has been praised for her vibrant writing style that uses beautiful intense imagery to build the worlds of her characters. When not pursuing her passion for writing, she enjoys gardening, traveling and listening to smooth jazz music.

Website: www.adahkennonauthor.com

Facebook:
https://www.facebook.com/search/top?q=adahkennonauthor

Also by Adah F. Kennon

TWIN FLAME MYSTERIES: THE NICHE

PATIENT OR PROFIT? WHERE IS THE LOVE?